And before she realised it

A Novel

Piroja Shroff

notionpress
.com

INDIA · SINGAPORE · MALAYSIA

ISBN 979-8-88555-971-3

CONTENTS

Contents

FOREWARD

Art imitates life. And mine definitely has.

I grew up in Mumbai, India, in a family very similar to Nadia's. I was the shy, lonely kid at school who never really fit in and tried hard every day to be part of the 'cool kids'. I am the girl who still struggles with the urge to push away love, friendships and any real intimacy because I'm so afraid of loss. Better not to have it than lose it later. All or nothing. (I'm working on this though). I went to NYC for my Master's Degree and then moved back to Mumbai to work, love and live. My 'the one' isn't named Arjun.

Not every incident in the book is true, but all the feelings are. I didn't write about a single thing I couldn't or didn't feel myself.

That's what made writing this book challenging and exhilarating for me. I would go to bed at night with anxiety because the next day I wanted to write about something I had never shared before. I worried about how my family would take the book and whether I was doing the people I most care about, a great disservice. But I ploughed through and fought with myself to become the person I want to be – honest and okay with being seen.

After every page where I revealed more of my own life, the joy, pain, struggles, love, secrets and what kept me going – My best friend – G, I felt an odd sensation. Through the shivers, I felt an inner calm. For it's all out there now and I can let the mask drop away. Here I am. See me. Read me. Now you know me. Phew!

I hope the book makes you feel.

"We choose our joys and our sorrows long before we experience them." – Kahlil Gibran

CHAPTER 1

HOMECOMING

There is a distinct muffled sound like a combination of ocean waves, mixed with a distant dhup dhuping heartbeat. Hearing this familiar sound once more, Nadia slowly realised where she was.

"Ohhhh…Yayyyyy!!!" she thought excitedly, "So much fun."

"Thanks G," she said with a smile, knowing He had done her a solid. She was, once again, in her mother's womb – cosy, unfettered, wise.

And as she fully wrapped her foetal mind around this information, she was filled with a bubbling anticipation for her second chance at this life; her Reset.

Resets were rarely granted, but Nadia knew the terms. She was being born to the same parents, in the same circumstances, to live and learn the same stuff, as Nadia, a second time round. *This time I'll definitely get it right*, she told herself.

In the meanwhile though, she was in for a nine month vacation. Being a foetus has its perks.

The moment she was birthed, she knew, it would be pandemonium! She would cry, gasp for air, and be inundated by the sounds of the world. And all the ever-growing earthly stimuli, would, eventually, make her forget her time in the womb, her previous lives, and most of the time, even her reason for taking birth. Every soul does.

So, Nadia made the most of this time and got into the womb zone. Ahh bliss!

***

On 11th May, Nadia knew her womb time was up. It was the first of many birthdays.

Sure enough, her world started tightening. She could hear mom's heartbeat hasten and breath, become loud. Mom was having her contractions and it was just a matter of time now. So, Nadia got ready for this inevitable voyage.

She felt like Magellan, ready to explore the seven seas and see for himself if the earth was actually round. She knew, just like he probably had, that there would be cyclones along the way and his ship may even come close to capsizing a couple of times, but the adventure of it all, made it worth it.

What could be more exciting than…life. What could be more of an adventure? Nadia was ready.

Here we go, she thought as she began to slide out. Mom was doing most of the work for now and Nadia tried to remain calm-ish and be pushed out.

Her surroundings drastically changed and in an altering minute, she was out. She knew the drill – she took a deep breath in, her first in nine months and yelled out "Hello world. We meet again," but to everyone around her it just sounded like, "Wahhhh waahhhh wahhh."

She needed to work on her articulation in the months to come.

***

And Nadia did – she worked on a great many things – object permanence, speech, walking, pooping in a designated area, writing, reading, holding her pee in through the night (this one took some time), managing all the emotions she felt and understanding all the people in her life, to name a few.

The central figure of Nadia's childhood was of course her mother. Her source. Mom was always in a hurry. Nadia's baby steps just couldn't run fast enough though, and mom was always three steps ahead, just out of arms' reach. Like Tom and Jerry.

So, when Mom was free, like at night before bed, or on some Sundays when they ran errands together, Nadia clung. She clung to her source, her sun. She clung onto her mother's soft arm as much as she could, afraid to let go for fear that Mom may run along. To four-year-old Nadia, nobody was cooler than her mother. Nobody's skin felt softer. Daddy's was all hairy. There was nobody Nadia wanted to spend more time with. There was nobody who

Nadia wanted more affection from. Nobody she could fathom feeling more love for.

And there was also nobody who seemed more irritated by her.

"I have work to do, Nadia! Do you think your father is going to do any of this when he gets home? You're just like him. Always creating more work for me."

Slap!

"I think you like to embarrass me, don't you? Such a sly girl. Crying in front of Granny so she thinks I'm a bad mother."

"No Ma. I...I'm sorry."

Her left cheek stung form the sharp slap planted on it for the crayons she had left on the floor that evening. She felt the warm tears slide down her cheeks as she told herself to pick up her crayons the next day or Mom would get angry again. She tried to control the tears, suck them back in. She really wished they wouldn't fall, as they bugged Mom the most, but her eyes didn't listen to her. As they reached her mouth though, she licked some of their salty shame up.

Crying child = more nuisance.

And Nadia knew it. If there was one thing she desperately didn't want to be, it was a bother. Mom had enough work already, she knew.

At four, Nadia could understand very little. Many things confused her, like why she couldn't go play in the park across the street? She could see it from her window and if nobody could take her, why couldn't she just toddle over herself?

Or how they slept at one in the night, but Daddy came home from work at ten. Isn't one before ten?

Or why Mom didn't like to be touched, when Nadia liked it quite a bit. Hugs were her favourite thing. Closely followed by chocolate cake and Thumbs Up.

Or why she couldn't watch TV with her parents at dinner time? She would eat with the maid in the dining room, while Mom and Dad ate in the bedroom, eyes transfixed on the TV.

Sometimes Nadia would finish her food quickly and while the maid washed the dishes, she would sneak up to the door of her parent's bedroom that stood ajar and watch TV with them. But she was careful to stand outside, quietly, so they wouldn't know she was there. There was nothing else for her to do really. Nadia had explored the whole house several times before, and she couldn't read too well yet. So, the nights were boring. At least in the morning there was school with lots of people to talk to. After school there was the crèche that had other kids in it too.

But once Nadia was picked up from the crèche at dark by Mom, then it was all boring-quiet time. Everything in their house was done in silence – Nadia ate dinner in silence, bathed in silence and quietly walked around the house while Mom and Dad watched TV. Then it was beddy time and she had to fall asleep. What a yawn fest!

One night, while lying in bed, Nadia recalled a conversation she had had that day in school with the new kid who spoke in a funny way. He had told her that there was this man who was everywhere and saw everything, so they mustn't do anything bad. "God is always watching," the boy said with a shudder, seeming a little afraid and confused, all at the same time.

Nadia wondered about this guy who supposedly watched them all.

How can this God watch us all, all the time? Is he like Santa? And Santa gives us gifts. What does this God give?

So on that night, Nadia decided to ask because if God is always around, he will hear the question.

Okay here goes: Hi God. My name is Nadia. Are you always watching me?

Nobody replied.

Oh….and why?

Still no reply.

I knew that new boy is dhaaping.

And Nadia cuddled her Eeyore stuffed toy and slowly sailed off to asleep.

But a strange thing started to happen as a few nights passed. Nadia started speaking to 'G' (her nickname for this God guy), in the night while she lay awake in bed.

Maybe it was to lessen her 'only child' loneliness (like an imaginary friend), maybe it was to feel less afraid of the dark room she slept in by herself, or maybe it was comforting to know that she had someone with her, always. But after a mostly silent evening at home, Nadia would speak to G every single night and then fall asleep with a *Sweet dreams G. Don't let the beddy bugs bite.*

"Sweet Dreams Nadia," G replied, though her earthly ears never heard him.

***

On the rare occasion that Daddy invited some friends over for dinner, they ate on the dining table together, and the silence of the night was broken. But even on those days, Nadia was told in advance, several times, by both her parents, to be quiet and behave herself.

"Don't embarrass me in front of the guests today or you see what I do to you," Mom whispered to her for the final time with her eyes bulging, just before she opened the door to let the guests in that night. Nadia knew those eyes and that hiss-like tone meant business, slightly comical as they seemed to her.

Mom looks like Dastardly from TV when she does that.

To behave, Nadia usually played a game of statue in her head. But, being five, she soon forgot about the game and blurted out:

"Daddy, can I help Gulabo make the biryani next time?" Her father mounted the saliva inducing biryani

15

their cook had made, onto her plate while laughing at something his friends Raj uncle and Rita aunty, had just said.

"What…Oh ummm no Nadia. That's not your job."

Everyone at the table laughed and Rita aunty mouthed an "Awww."

"But I love the smell in the kitchen and…"

But Akbar cut her off and turning to his wife for the first time that night, he said, "And Roxanne, why is Nadia wearing those ugly glasses?"

"Baby, go take off your glasses before starting dinner. Let aunty and uncle see how pretty you are."

She got up and obeyed, noticing a glare from Mom. Mom had told her to take off her pink glasses before the guests arrived and she had forgotten.

Nadia knew that something about this request made her feel an ouch in her chest but she didn't know why.

After that, all through dinner, she didn't utter a word and ate with her eyes fixed on her plate. Over the years she would become very good at shutting the world out of her mind to avoid that ouch feeling.

I wish I could become invisible, like the Cheshire Cat can. He can just turn it off and on for fun.

Everyone else ate and conversed and praised the truly delicious biryani. Occasionally, they looked at the pretty, well-behaved and noiseless child sitting at the table. The dinner party was picture perfect.

***

Over the next couple of years, Nadia grew into a young girl. Innocent, shallow, stubborn and full of hope, with all her life ahead of her and many, many things yet to learn. By fifteen, she had pitch black straight hair, sharp doe-like eyes framed by bushy eyebrows and long eyelashes, braces, now green glasses, a gawky-lanky-skinny body and a nose she would one day grown into, but hadn't yet.

Every morning, she sat in front of the mirror and conducted her hair brushing ritual. Then she quickly rushed out of the house for her fifteen minute walk to school.

On that day, Nadia walked along Marine Drive on the water front humming a Backstreet Boys' song. The noise, traffic and general boom-booming of the hot Mumbai morning was all around her. Sweat clung to her skin that day, like it did every day in Mumbai, as the harsh Indian sun shone down, reflecting heat off the road. The grey waves crashed against the boulders beyond the promenade to her right, as the subtle smell of dog and/or human pee filled the air. Yet, she was oblivious to it all, listening to her Sony Discman which granny had gifted her and going over her wardrobe choices in her head. She had a birthday party to attend that night.

I'll wear my new strappy blue dress, she decided, trying to keep up with all the 'cool girls' and their overflowing closets.

Popularity, and fitting in were her goals for the year. And if they were achieved, then she would wish for a cute boyfriend and a new Motorola Razor cell phone, as well. Baby steps.

In those free moments walking to school each morning, Nadia often fixated on her own personal dramas – *Why me God? Why is my life so tough? Rhea has clear skin... Pooja's parents love her sooo much... Zara is head-girl... Neha is the most popular girl in school... I look like an overgrown koala bear! What about me?? Why can't you cut me some slack once in a while...*

G and The helper smiled because that was the day!

"Her 'slack' is on his way," The helper confirmed.

It was their first encounter. Arjun came to her school that day to give a speech on swimming. He had just been selected to represent their state-Maharashtra, in the 'Under 16' category and Gandhi Academy wanted to promote sports in their school. So, as part of the Young Go-Getter segment of that month's assembly, he arrived.

He spoke clearly, confidently and with a tinge of arrogance in his deep voice. He had a shaved head, as all serious swimmers do, with broad shoulders that particularly stuck out because he was so darned thin. His almond-shaped dark eyes complimented his swimmers' tan perfectly. His face was all eyes and dimples; nothing else could compete with the prominence of those two features. She listened to his speech, and thought, *Whoaa!! This kid works hard man! I wonder where that kind of passion comes from?*

That was The helper's cue. She is ready! She recognised passion and was wondering about it. Bam!

Suddenly, the teacher sitting closest to Nadia gestured to her "Give him this bouquet once he is finished and everyone starts clapping, okay?"

"Okay Miss!" Nadia said, while thinking:

Oh nooo! I'm going to have to go up on stage in front of the whole school! How embarrassing... I'm not waxed!!! I hope nobody notices my hairy legs... although how could they not. Ughhh this is such a nightmare. Lazy fricking teacher! Couldn't she just give him the bouquet herself.

But too late.

He was done speaking and everyone began to clap. She nervously got up and went onto the stage. Climbing the stairs, she noticed his eyes on her. *Hmmm he is kind of cute, even with the whole sadhu-shaved-head look.*

As if he had read her mind, Arjun smiled at her.

His smile and dimples on both cheeks, sent her into an instant, insecure panic.

Ohhh shit! Do I smile back? Is it too late now? Soooo awkward. Her mind scrambled as she felt a hot blush spread over her pimpled cheeks.

She handed him the bouquet while trying to avoid his gaze. However, he was one step ahead of her. He put out his hand and said, "Thanks. I'm Arjun."

"Uhhh you're welcome."

She turned and sprinted off stage, without shaking his hand. That was more interaction with a cute dimpled boy than her shyness could handle.

Why am I such a nervous klutz? she thought. *I should have at least told him my name. Now he will think that I'm a snob.*

And he kinda did.

The school day ended and soon they both forgot about each other. He was that odd boy who smiled and disarmed her, and she was that snobby Gandhi Academy girl.

But she had taken what she really needed to from that first encounter – passion can be an anchor. And Nadia really needed something to hold her steady. Not fully knowing why, she began to work harder and harder at school.

The helper had noticed her noticing Arjun's passion. That was step one.

"Step one done so quick?" G said with surprise at Nadia's progress.

"But she still hasn' t seen the value in loving herself. Let' s give her more time to figure that step out," G said after a moment, never one to rush things.

"I' m on it," The helper replied, utterly focussed on his job, "I' ll sprinkle her days with chances to pick it up, like we did the first time. Before the Reset."

"Yup. Try till she sees...but don' t be too harsh with the lessons, okay?" A hint of worry for Nadia, apparent in G' s voice.

"Yes , Yes! I remember..." The helper laughed, "Baby steps."

***

Pushing herself made everything else easier somehow. It helped to distract her from the daily fights her mom and dad were having and it even helped block out the isolation Nadia was faced with at school.

Home was slowly becoming an emotional war zone, full of long periods of sub-zero silence and then sudden eruptions of the most vicious kind between Akbar and Roxanne.

"You're a f*****g bi**h!"

"You coward. Grow a pair sometime soon please and your daughter may respect you someday. Once a mamma's boy, always a mamma's boy."

21

"Don't speak about Mumma like that. I should have listened when they all told me —'Roxanne is a selfish woman.' But I was blinded by youth, I guess."

"Oh please!! What youth are you talking about, Akbar? I never witnessed any signs of it. You never had any passion, spark, or charm. What was I thinking when I married you. You have wasted my life. I stopped loving you a long time ago, Akbar."

"I *never* loved you, Roxanne!"

Nadia had a morbid curiosity for hearing their fights. She would press her ear against their bedroom door and listen. They were putting on a show and she would be their audience, as excruciating and puke-worthy as it was.

Due to their intensifying battles, their neglect for Nadia had also heightened. Days went by without either of them so much as checking in on Nadia's life. She was alive, she went to school, she came home, and that was enough for them. Amidst all this, studying gave her an escape.

By now her mind could successfully tune out, what her heart couldn't. And as much as the conflict and neglect hurt her, it also pushed her towards coming up with an escape plan. Her sole aim became — *I got to study hard, get top grades, get into a university abroad and get out of this house. Sweet escape!*

An ocean between her and her parents, would surely make her feel rosy and happy, right?

Their hostility for each other and apathy for her, wouldn't affect her anymore, once she was in another country, right?

Or, at least, it will make them eventually miss me and pay attention to me, right?

She was still too young to know – you cannot outrun your reality.

CHAPTER 2

THE SCHOOL OF LIFE

Like many teenagers before her, Nadia, from the fledgling ages of fifteen to eighteen, believed the damaging triad – I must be liked. I must be cool. I must keep trying to be liked and cool.

That is why Nadia remembers her last four years of High School at Gandhi Academy as 'The Misfit Era'. During high school, Nadia was…different. And in high school, there is no bigger taboo! She read a little too much, she was shy, gawky and didn't belong to the same wealth level, religion or mind-set as most of the kids at Gandhi Academy. Not to mention, by the time she was sixteen, everyone knew her parents were getting a divorce. And in the India of the early 2000s, there was no bigger taboo.

Even an alien from Saturn could have fitted in better than she did.

At Nadia's school, there was the crew of rich kids, who were not only characterised by the clothes they wore, vacations they took, fancy cars they came to school in, kitty-parties their moms attended and gadgets they owned, but also by their main feature – they were, by default, COOL.

And Nadia, by default, was extremely jealous of them. Duhh!

They said things like:

"If I get above eighty in my exams, my dad has promised to buy me a BMW when I turn eighteen." Or:

"My mum isn't bringing a hot lunch for me to school today so she gave me Rs. 500 to eat in the canteen." Or:

"My math tutor charges 200,000 Rupees a year. I'll for sure ace the exam."

And Nadia thought things like:

I better get above eighty-five in my exams or I'll be an even bigger loser. And:

Hot lunch at school? Mom and Dad don't even eat dinner with me most days. And:

My monthly pocket money is Rs. 400 and any half decent gift is double that amount. How am I going to buy Arya a gift for her birthday? Maybe I should just skip her party. And:

I wish I could also afford this math tutor, maybe then I could become a part of the cool group. Maybe then we can become friends.

Her skewed definition of friends and desperate yearning to be in the 'in crowd' at school, made Nadia create and fervently pursue the adolescent girl's Mission Impossible – becoming one of 'them'.

But, day after day, month after month, despite the *Mission Impossible* theme music playing in her head, Nadia's mission remained – impossible.

Duhh.

The only thing she gained from all that incessant trying, was a mist of anger.

"Why won't they just let me in? They always make me feel like an outsider," Nadia bitched to Payal one day, on their bi-weekly evening walk. Payal was her neighbour and friend who studied at another school and so was removed from the Gandhi Academy drama.

The helper, always present, knew the truth behind her words – she was not angry at them. But at herself.

G was using his old faithful, school drama, to prepare Nadia for life, for pain, and for letting go.

This was her 'microcosm practice', before entering the real world. It was meant to teach her that it takes two hands to clap, and every time the 'cool girls' did anything to show Nadia that she wasn't one of them, she would clap back, by trying that much harder. If only she had stopped her end of the clap… If only she had known that it was possible to stop.

But learn it she did, that Friday morning, in the 11th grade.

Nadia vividly remembers the day of the Nine Months To Go incident, the way all personality-altering traumas are glued into one's memory.

It started off like any other normal school day, dull and noisy. It was Thursday morning and Nadia was sitting in her seat next to Siya, a girl who was part of the 'cool gang' but had never been directly mean to Nadia before. It was second period and their Geography teacher hadn't entered the class yet. While they waited for the teacher to arrive, out of nowhere, Siya turned to Nadia, and casually inquired, "I heard you are pregnant. What did your parents say?"

Nadia heard the words, felt the word slap, and then, FROZE.

Mouth frozen.

Eyes frozen.

Toes frozen.

Hair frozen.

World frozen.

Pregnant. How. I am seventeen. I just had my first kiss, last month. What. Who said that? Why. Who believed that? Who spread that? Who causally asks that? Have my parents heard this lie? Why can't I respond? she screamed in her brain. She never said it out loud though, as her tongue too was frozen.

And then, after what seemed like too many mute seconds, like every frozen thing, Nadia started to thaw. And the gush began from her eyes, nose and heart.

She ran to the bathroom and wailed, bent over as if in physical pain. She was utterly shocked and confused by the plain mean lie that had just been thrown at her.

After a ten-minute bathroom breakdown, however, Nadia had to head back to class. The world hadn't actually frozen and Nadia had to return to World Standard Time.

The teacher, who had since arrived, asked her where she had gone and why she was late for second period. She had no answer. She got yelled at by the teacher for this but her ears were still a little icy, and the yelling didn't seep in. Thank God for small mercies.

Siya looked down or directly at the teacher, the rest of the day. Clearly, she hadn't expected Nadia to cry, at least not in front of her, and it had thrown her off.

After school that day, Nadia rushed home and cried quietly in bed till 6 pm sharp. That was when Mom got home from work, so Nadia washed her face of the frozen pain, and made sure she appeared normal when her mother opened the door to enter the house that evening.

How could she explain such an embarrassing lie to anyone? She was too too too ashamed, knowing what everyone at school thought about her.

And how could she bring herself to repeat the mean words that had bitten her heart to anyone, least of all her mother.

But Siya had said it. Causally. Nonchalantly.

The girls who had invented it, had said it. Viciously. Nonchalantly.

And now Nadia just had to take it. Quietly. Icily.

That night, long after everyone had gone to bed, Nadia made herself some chicken noodle soup for the soul. Then, she sat down with her cuppa, to calculate with a new resolve in her heart- How many shitty days left for shitty high school to end?

Coincidently, she found that, after all the weekends, study leave and holidays were deducted, Nadia had exactly 275 days of school left. Approximately nine months.

Cosmic irony much?

Only 275 days to go, she told herself, which made her feel a little calmer. *I can do it if I take it one day at a time. Baby steps!*

And the *Mission Impossible* theme music started playing in her head once again. This mission, she would accomplish.

The next morning, when Nadia awoke from her oddly restful night's sleep, (courtesy G) she knew what she had to do. Let GO!

And so, for the last nine months of school, she didn't try to fit in or be liked by the 'cool girls'. She had written it all off in that awaking moment on Friday morning. And even a poem on the subject streamed out of Nadia's pen into her journal.

"Now you can figure out who you really are," G said, glad the school-drama period was coming to an end; glad that Nadia had stopped her end of the clap. Mission accomplished.

Jungle Grapes and Other Shapes
By Nadia

Boxes keep us protected,
From the feeding frenzy that is school.
Like a school of fish swim safer together,
Safety in packs is nature's rule.

So I ask, can I enter your box?
I promise I'll be cool.
No box, means social isolation.
We need each other to survive.
The lone zebra never makes it.
The lioness rips its throats out; the vulture
picks at its eye.

Can I enter your box, I ask?
How much harder do you want me to try?

The box will be my mould.
Into which I'll fit; I'll finally belong.
The box will help me get through school.
It's not like I have anything else going on.

Can I enter your box, I beg?
In the jungle, only boxes make you strong.

Don't worry, I see the irony.
I'm not delusional, you know.
If everyone were inside the box,
Then no one would be left out alone.

May I enter your box, I persist?
Don't be mean; Throw me a bone.

But hold up, what am I saying?
Your box is just a square.
And maybe I'm a rhombus!
Maybe there is no need to despair.

Maybe I can't be that shape.
And maybe that's just fine!
'Sour Grapes' is what you will call it,
I call it - reclaiming the shape that's mine!

*** *

The conveyor belt continued moving, and Nadia moved with it. School ended soon after, and she fulfilled her one aim, acing her finals! The ten-hour study days, staying out of the kitchen and chained to her desk had paid off.

I get to leave home. Yipeeee.

She had gotten into some decent schools and chose Boston City University as it was one of the three schools that gave her financial aid, but more importantly, she needed to be in a city. She knew that small American towns would drive her mad, for she had grown up in one of the most populated and hurried cities on earth. The rush and buzz were now in her blood.

She started University that September and neither her Mom nor Dad accompanied her to Boston to help her set up in this foreign country – Work was too busy, they had both said. Besides, "You are such a strong and independent girl. You can handle it, right?" Mom insisted, as dad had sat by quietly. Granny had looked at her son and ex-daughter in law with pursed lips and said in a huff that she would go with Nadia. But Nadia knew that the flight across the ocean would be just too much for Granny's arthritic knees. So at eighteen, Nadia had handled it alone, because she had to.

This move to another continent, came with an almost instantaneous mental and emotional paradigm shift. The sudden independence and fresh start worked its magic on Nadia.

At university, her shyness, that had been her armour to keep the world out, started slipping off. She stopped taking her every move so seriously. Nobody was watching. It was okay to just be. And so, she actually started connecting with people, making friends – it began with her roommates.

Isla R was a light-haired Texan, who loved romantic movies, travelling, exercise and was getting her masters in Psychology. She sat by the living room window in their shared apartment and read books on the Oedipus complex and other bizarre conversation starters, for hours on end. Nadia and she bonded over their shared love for spicy food and made Taco Night a weekly tradition in their campus apartment – No. 122.

This was the first time Nadia was living with people who ate dinner together at least once a week.

Tara Deluca, the third inhabitant of flat no. 122, was from Boston and had the full-blown Boston accent Nadia had only ever heard before, in movies. Tara sang all day and was studying business studies, just like Nadia. Their bond was slow to begin, and was built steadily over the next four years of college. They had many of the same classes and even joined the Oceanography Club together. A flyer somewhere spoke of extra credit and they figured that they could get in some sun and tan-time while 'working', so why not.

At Oceanography Club, the more Nadia read, and the more she listened in (passively at first) to the discussions about the state of our marine life and the grave danger our oceans are in, the more she wanted to get involved, make a difference. Slowly but surely, her passion deepened in her… and it pushed her to evolve.

Nadia found herself feeling passionate about life, passionate about doing well in her classes and passionate about the Oceanography Club.

She was now, slowly, becoming the 'Nadia' she needed to become. The Nadia that had lay dormant inside her, beneath the mish-mash of everything and everyone else. She now was starting to realise what she liked and more importantly what she disliked. She was forming her own views: distinct and definite.

Confidence is an amazing thing, she thought, one evening as she walked home from a Charles River clean-up drive. *I wish I could've learnt it in school, instead of Chemistry and Trigonometry.*

Sadly, only the school of life provides *real* education.

CHAPTER 3

PRACTICE MAKES PERFECT

One day, Nadia crossed paths with him again. It was their second encounter – the 25th of November.

The air was more than a little nippy and she was heading home from the library to curl up in her warm and cosy bed to do her final paper before Thanksgiving break. And then she saw him. He was jogging; unconcerned and carefree. As if it was absolutely natural to wear shorts on a November day in Boston.

He looked at her and there it was again… that smile. Those dimples. This time however, she smiled back.

Maybe it was because he looked absurd jogging in his little gym shorts and UnderArmour T-shirt, or maybe it was because she didn't feel awkward smiling at strangers anymore. But she smiled back, while they locked eyes for that brief couple of seconds, as they both continued on their way.

As soon as he had passed her, a glimmer of recognition dawned on Nadia. *Could he be that same guy from three years ago – the swimmer guy?* His head wasn't shaved anymore, but those eyes and that smile were unmistakeable. Unforgettable.

What's he doing here? she thought as she felt a small flutter in her tummy. His smile had once again disarmed her. But she pushed those thoughts aside knowing she probably wouldn't see him again.

Boston is huge! Plus these athlete types with their swimming and jogging are usually arrogant anyways. Okay, I need my warm bed now! Got to finish this paper before my date with Zack tonight.

The paper was a quick job. She had always been good at expressing her thoughts and opinions in writing. Speaking sometimes was a problem, but never writing. All her professors in fact, commended her on her written work.

"So eloquent! And especially coming from someone whose first language isn't English," they all said. She was tired of explaining to them that English *was* her first language. She was from Mumbai for god's sake! But to them, India was still the land of gurus, yoga and gang rape. Not necessarily in that order.

As Nadia put on her go-to date outfit – a black fitted sweater dress that showed off her curves but still seemed classy, and her newly purchased wedge heel boots, she felt the butterflies set in. *What if he thinks I'm boring? What if he stands me up? What if what if what if—*

The insecurities from her childhood still managed to creep up from time to time. Some things you just can't shake; but they were much quieter now.

At least she was glad she had outgrown her self-proclaimed 'ugly duckling meets koala bear' phase. She now considered herself attractive. She wasn't very tall, very curvy or extremely pretty. Her hair wasn't really silky, her nose wasn't delicate and her skin didn't glow. Her teeth weren't too straight and her smile wasn't exceptional. But she liked the way she looked. It all fit. It all felt right. She looked the way she was meant to.

At that point, she went over her pre-date self-confidence boosting chat with her more confident avatar in the mirror. The Beyoncé in Nadia looked into her eyes and said, "You are vibrant, fun and special. He will see that. No need to worry. He asked you out and he must have had a reason. You're a hottie! Don't worry. He is going to be so smitten with you by the end of it, that he won't know what hit him."

The mirror chats helped diffident Nadia, who started going over her arsenal of conversation starters in her head.

Some of the most used ammo included, "So where did you grow up? Are you close with your parents? Any siblings? What's on your travel bucket list for the year?" And if things were really going well… "What's the wildest thing you've ever done?"

She felt safe within these questions.

Talk less, listen more. No need to make yourself vulnerable by actually sharing a real piece of who you are. That's for over-sharers and needy people. Right?

***

Zack arrived to pick her up at ten minutes past eight. They had met at a two-day Charles River clean-up drive. Her Oceanography Club had organised the event and he had come with his surfer buddies. He was from California and had the sandy blonde hair she had always found extremely attractive. The surfer tan, the bored look in his eyes and the fact that he was 'All-American', did it for her. He was the exact opposite of what she had known all her life in Mumbai and so for some reason, she thought that he was somehow better, in the typical 'grass is greener' sense. If you have only ever eaten dhansak, wouldn't a cheeseburger seem like the meal you've been waiting for?

They walked to the diner on Boylston Street. She ordered pancakes (yes, for dinner) and he ordered the meat loaf. They made small talk and asked all the generic questions. Slowly, he started opening up a little… he had taken a surfing trip with his boys to Peru last year. He had two younger sisters and a spaniel named Rue. Speaking of… "Have you seen the show?" he asked.

"Euphoria? No I haven't started to yet," Nadia responded.

"You should come over sometime and watch with me," he said.

"Sure! I'm always on the lookout for some new show," she replied with a giggle. She knew what "come over to watch a show with me" was code for. Confident Nadia was doing the victory jig in her head.

After dinner, they shared dessert – a slice of apple pie (could it get more American?!), and he even fed her a bite. And then Zack walked her home as they shared his umbrella through the light drizzle that had begun. They hugged at the door and he said, "I had a great time. Can I see you again?"

"Yea definitely. I had a great time too," she said with a big smile but no flutter in her tummy.

"Okay great! I'll call you." And with that he was off. No kiss, which she found a little odd.

As soon as she entered their apartment, Isla, was there waiting for the scoop. Tara, was out with her 'man friend' Carlos. They refused to call each other boyfriend or girlfriend, even though they all knew that Tara wanted to.

So, Nadia dished to Isla. When she reached the 'no kiss' detail, Isla's eyebrows shot up. "WHAT? No kiss… he didn't even try? Are you sure it was a date? And you're sure it went well?"

"No. Yes. Yes. I think he just decided to hold off till next time. No need to overthink this, babe. Okay, I got to hit the sack now. I have Hackman at 8 am and he notices when people doze off in class. Chat more tomorrow?"

Isla agreed and walked into her own room to go to sleep with air-kisses aimed at Nadia.

Nadia entered her small dorm room with a single un-made bed, one cupboard that was filled to bursting point with all of Nadia's clothes and books, and a small desk that sat by the window. Below the bed were the three suitcases she had flown to Boston with, all her life's belongings packed into them.

As she closed her room door, she slowly noticed that she hadn't really *loved* her date with Zack. It had just been… okay-ish. But she still hoped he would call, of course.

I'm sure he will grow on me. I hope he liked me though…

G noticed her flip flop on Zack. "She is listening to her gut now but not acting on it."

It was time for a test. The helper obliged.

***

The next day there was no call from Zack. He didn't call the day after that, and the day after that. To say that she checked her phone on an hourly basis would not be an overstatement.

Why hasn't he called? This stupid three day rule! What should I do?

Even Nadia's mom and dad had met in college. She had heard the story a million times. Mom had gone up to Dad after class one day and asked him if he wanted to go to Jehangir Art Gallery with her. He was so flattered that a girl had asked him out, that it never occurred to him to tell her that he didn't know or care about art. In a sense, their first date was a perfect representation of their marriage. She took charge and he followed, but always for the wrong reasons.

It was five months before Nadia's 10th grade ICSE exam when her parents had finally decided to tell her about their upcoming divorce. Mom said that she and Nadia would be moving out. Dad would stay in the apartment Nadia had grown up in. Akbar never once asked Nadia to stay back with him. And this fact had made Nadia feel disposable, like her feelings on all of this, were utterly irrelevant. Like *she* was utterly irrelevant.

She felt as if to her father, she had come to represent an extension of Roxanne. And could you blame the guy for wanting a clean break? Yes, she could. And she did.

In the months leading up to the separation, when all the fights and trash-talk got too much at home, Nadia would call Sabina granny, Payal, or Jay, whom she dated for all of 10th grade. He was her first kiss. Their version of dating included secretly holding sweaty hands whenever they could, and staying on the phone for hours discussing riveting and profound topics like pizza or homework or their school's elections for head boy and head girl.

At that point in her life, Nadia was just glad to feel attention from *someone*, if not her parents. She knew she didn't *really* like him. She just liked the attention. And isn't that why everyone dates?

Doesn't attention = love?

Halfway into 11th grade, Jay broke up with Nadia. He liked Riana now.

And like teenage heartbreak usually does – it felt like the world had stopped rotating. No Jay=No rotation.

Frequent grilled cheese sandwiches, a lot of sleep and diving back into her studies helped Nadia slowly forget that first glimpse of heartbreak and ignore her parents' ongoing divorce. And one day, in a moment of rare insight, the lesson was clear to her – she had to learn to trust the voice inside.

She had chosen to ignore the fact that she hadn't *really* liked Jay, despite sort of always knowing it deep down.

Why did I even date him for over a year?

It had been so easy to ignore that soft voice inside. Especially since she was, at the time, sixteen, with Eminem playing on full volume on her Sony disc-man.

Even today, acting on her gut instinct, was precisely what she had to do with Zack. But could she?

***

Finally, five days later she got a text from Zack: "Hey. What's up?"

Relieved AF, she began composing her reply. Texting a boy was serious business. She didn't want to appear too needy. Feigning disinterest is key. Baby steps.

She waited a few hours, and sent the text, which she had typed out exactly seven minutes after reading his. They texted intermittently, back and forth for two hours and managed to say or ask nothing of any substance. He still hadn't even asked her on a second date and now the voice inside was getting louder and clearer.

Finally, she decided to do what she was learning to… trust her gut! His 'surfer boy hotness' had made her ignore her gut for a few days – cute boys and day dreams have a way of doing that sometimes. But now she remembered the vibe she got from him the first time they met and all through dinner too. She didn't *really* like him. It was just… meh.

Her eyes had briefly won over her gut that day, the latter being comparatively easy to ignore. But she realised it now.

Dang. I did it again. What a waste of breath. Why do I keep going for people I know I'm not genuinely into? I can read it, but I choose to try anyways.

The 'why' was in her DNA. Isn't that what her parents too had done? Isn't that what most people do?

"Why can't instinct come with a microphone and surround-sound? G, you really need to get more hi-tech," Nadia said addressing her forever friend.

G chuckled. "I'm trying, I'm trying…"

"Few more tests and she won't need the surround-sound," The helper chimed in.

She petered off the texting with Zack. It wasn't the right fit, but she turned to her journal instead, pen in hand.

Growing Louder
By Nadia

Yesterday,
I cursed the silence,
I felt alone and forgotten.

Tonight,
My own voice greets me,
And I remember to listen.

Now,
I am all the sound I need.
My heartbeat and me;
Friends eternally.

***

A week later, she met a new friend for a quick bite between classes. Chris had been chatty and helpful at every Oceanography Club meeting, but she had never initiated a hang-out before. Initiating was something she would work on for years to come; vulnerability felt unsafe. But at least she could see it now.

Christopher Nunes was 6'1, with an athletic build, a chin dimple, shaggy brown hair that was always a bit too dishevelled and light green eyes lined with dark eyebrows and eyelashes. There was no doubt about it – he was handsome! But he too, like Nadia, had a palpable shyness.

Luckily however, they struck up a conversation about chicken wings and easily enough, the plan to meet and eat, was formed. It was definitely not a date though, and for that she was glad. This time, she consciously looked out for how she felt around Chris.

She felt like laughing. And relaxed. Both very good signs.

"She noticed!!" The helper declared triumphantly as G smiled.

At lunch, they talked about Chris's home in a small town in Mexico, his daily phone calls with his mom and dad who missed him intensely, her meh dating history, the classes they were currently taking, Chris's love for camping and the outdoors, Nadia's love for the ocean and cooking and on and on.

After lunch, he walked her to class, texted her that night, they made plans for the weekend… and just like that, Nadia let him into her world.

***

"Do you add ketchup to the mince?" Chris asked while stirring the minced meat around the pan as per the instructions Nadia had given him.

Isla was making dessert-smoothies for them all. Tara and Carlos laid the table while Nadia mixed the salad.

"Yea, use this spicy one I got from home."

"Mmmm….It's yummy. Get me a bottle next time you visit home." Chris said after tasting the chillies in it.

Nadia just nodded. She had no intention of going home any time soon.

But maybe I can get him a bottle from the Patel Brothers shop.

After her move to Boston, Mom and dad hadn't become any more communicative with her, as she had secretly hoped. Mom spoke to her in a rush-rush tone whenever Nadia called her, then would say she was extremely busy and hang up within 6 minutes. Seven at the most. Dad was a bit better. He asked Nadia how the weather was, how her grades were, update her on Indian politics and then hand the phone to Sabina granny who had moved in with him recently. Old age and all.

But suddenly the aromas of the room caught Nadia's attention and pulled her out of her self-pity rabbit hole. She took the smells in and looked around her. For a second, she felt like she was looking at her life from the outside, and she realised that she liked what she saw. She saw herself smiling while she mixed the greens in that big brown bowl. She saw Chris and Isla joke with each other as they always did. Their friendship too had developed easily and quickly. She saw Tara and Carlos take a seat at the table set for five. She felt her mouth start to water a little at the familiar smell of apartment 122 tacos and then she felt it all sink in.

I am here. This is my now. I'm happy.

She smiled even bigger now. The food was ready and they all sat down for Sunday dinner, just like they had done for the past few weeks.

G and The helper smiled too.

CHAPTER 4

SILVER LININGS

The final year of university comes with its own generous dollop of stress. Final submission stress, job hunting stress, moving away from your friend's stress, knowing that the best four years of your life are soon coming to an end stress, and most importantly, the stress of the unknown.

She hid it well, but Nadia's heart was constantly thudding with insecurities. *What if I don't get a job here? What if I have to move back to Mumbai? What if all the student loans have been a waste? What if I lose touch with all my friends? What if I'm never this happy, ever again?* The humorous paradox of losing her happiness to worrying about losing her happiness, was obviously lost on Nadia.

By January, she had submitted all her job applications and devised her plan B and C, in case she didn't get a job in the US. Plan B would be to take out another student loan and enrol in a Master's program. It wasn't ideal, BUT it would keep her in the US for another two to three years at the least. Plan C would be to curl up, wail for a few days, and then bite the bullet and apply for jobs in Canada. She figured some country in the western hemisphere, is better than going back home to her family and old life. Little did she know, destiny would take her home sooner or later. Nobody can run forever.

All this worry and anxiety about the scary, unknown F word – Future, eventually took its toll and by February, after a good three months of intense heart thumping, Nadia fell sick.

Ughhhh. Why me God? I don't have the time or energy for this. I can't be sick right now.

Being sick during this busy month was made even more agonising by the fact that everyone else too was busy, busy, busy. Nobody had time to help. Nobody had time to play caregiver. Nadia didn't have the heart to even ask.

I can't intrude on someone like that, especially right now. Asking for help is too needy.

"It' s time to begin to teach her to voice her needs," G decided.

The helper agreed, "Okay. I' ll get started on it."

***

For two looong, tiring, phlegm filled weeks, Nadia's flu didn't go away. It only steadily worsened. Even after the doctor at the student health centre prescribed her some strong-ass meds, the flu valiantly fought on as Nadia began inching closer to breakdown point. By the end of week two, she was so weak that she would spontaneously start to cry and had even run out of food at home. She was too sick to do a grocery store run and after starving for a full day, she finally cracked and called up Chris. She knew he didn't have class on Mondays.

"Hey. Listen… I'm really sorry to bother you like this. I know you're probably busy with studying and all… but I don't know what else to do."

"What's wrong?" Chris immediately asked, alarm apparent in his voice.

"I'm sick… and I need a favour please… I'm out of food at home and literally can't get out of bed. Could you please do a grocery run for me. I'll pay you of course. Please."

"Wow, three pleases huh! Yeah, no worries. Text me all the stuff you need."

"Okay thanks a lot!"

"By the way, have you been to the doc? What meds are you taking?"

"I've been twice already ya but the antibiotics don't seem to be working. I've been on them for ten days now."

"What? That's why you've been MIA for two weeks now? What do you have?"

"Oh, it's just the flu. No biggie."

"Nadia you haven't gotten well after taking antibiotics for ten days!! That's a big freaking deal. Why didn't you call me sooner? I could've helped."

His irritation was apparent as his voice rose higher than its normal volume.

"I'm okay. Really! I didn't want to bother you."

"Jeez…What are friends for bro…"

This left Nadia stunned. She didn't respond. She had never thought of it that way.

Wait… so friendships are about… help?

They are not just for swapping dating problems, gossip and having fun with the person?

Isn't asking for help, too much?

Who does that?

Breaking the silence, Chris finally said, "Okay anyways, I'll be there soon. Text me the grocery and medication list."

"Okay, I am texting it to you right now. Thank you." And with that they hung up.

Forty minutes later, Chris rushed in, put all the grocery bags down and felt her forehead. She was burning up and must have looked noticeably frail which sent Chris into full blown nurse-mode. Nadia had never seen him like this and usually would've joked about it, if she had had the energy.

"First, go take a cool shower, don't lock the bathroom door in case you faint, then get straight into bed. I'm going to make you some food in the meantime."

"But… there's no need… I can just pay you for the groceries and…"

"Shower. Cool water. Now."

Chris's new-found bossiness worked. Nadia didn't try and argue anymore. She just did as he said, too worn out to refuse the help.

Chris stayed till nine that night. He cooked her the comfort food she had so often made for him- chicken noodle soup, put Gatorade by her bedside, and then once she fell asleep, he left. He returned the next day after his classes to check in on her. He stayed in the 'Nurse Chris' avatar for the next three days, while Nadia got better and better.

Isla and Tara alternated cooking meals for Nadia, while she recuperated.

Nadia, of course, hadn't even told her roommates that she was sick. They had just assumed she was holed up in her room studying, as she always did before exam week.

They are busy with life, boyfriends, homework and studying, she had reasoned; *no point in making a fuss!*

They had found out from Chris and scolded Nadia for her silliness.

"I can't believe you were right under our noses and you didn't tell us for this long, babe," Tara said.

"You're like a sickness ninja," Isla joked.

Nadia's ninja like ability to hide her needs came from her experiences growing up, which had taught her to be as 'need-free' as possible. Needy kid = irritating kid, she had learned! Ain't nobody got time for 'babying'. Mom and Dad are busy and have problems of their own to deal with, she had learned. And to unlearn something is harder than it seems.

But as the fever and weakness lifted, and she could think clearly again, Nadia wished she had reached out sooner.

She began to realise that she had people in her life she could genuinely reach-out to now.

Ahhh silver linings Nadia thought, as the dark cloud of flu began to pass.

G and The helper high fived. Wearing her down had worked this time. The message had been received.

***

Before Nadia knew it, exams came and went. She graduated and was glad that the studying phase of her life was over, once and for all. Now time to 'adult'.

But unknown to Nadia, the school of life was just getting started with her. G's plan was meandering onward.

CHAPTER 5

THE CALM

Plan A worked out and it was what dreams were made of. Nadia moved to New York City after her graduation for an internship with eWay, that she hoped would turn into a well-paying job in six months. Fun city, fun internship that could turn into a job, fun friends nearby and all her life ahead of her.

Finally…it's my time now!

She lived near Cooper Union, in a tiny apartment with two other girls she had met through a broker. Chris lived in Chelsea with his cousin who worked on Wall Street. Tara got a job in Boston, and Isla was moving to NYC in a couple of months to start her PHD at Columbia.

In her first six months in NYC, eWay hired Nadia full time. She started earning and doing extremely adult things like saving money, filing her tax returns and paying off her student loans. Big girl time.

And big girls need rituals. Hers became girls night once a week with her roommates and Gabby, Chris' new girlfriend, and an RV adventure with Chris one weekend every two months or so. He kept it parked in Queens outside the house of yet another cousin (Mexicans are very well-connected people!). They would take the subway to Queens and then pick up the RV to embark on their game of 'discover'.

Sometimes they would plan their destination in advance – a pretty beach in the Hamptons, Coney island, the Cloisters, Jersey… once they even drove all the way up to the Canadian border for the weekend! So many adventures to have, and so little time to have them. But most of the time it was pure spontaneity, or at least their version of it.

"Turn right here, oh this street looks pretty."

"I wonder how long, Long Island really is?" And so on.

And for the next two years, through job changes, roommate drama, telephonic fights with Mom and/or Dad, and the occasional bouts of homesickness, Chris was her rock.

Thanks G for such a great support system. Nadia would often think.

Life was a happy collage of work, eating take-out from all the assorted cuisines NYC has to offer, intermittent dating, girl's nights, cleaning her apartment, Chris, and the rare trip back to Mumbai to visit her family.

Of course, her parents thought Chris was gay. How can a boy and a girl be 'just friends'? How can attraction truly not be part of the equation? Unfathomable! That kind of platonic thing was only for Plato. And wasn't he gay too?

While she was visiting home, Nadia's Dad said to her, over a strained dinner that had already gone on past their usual crisp one-hour meeting, "Be careful of these homo types. It is best to stay away from people like that."

Nadia knew her dad was a bit conservative in an Indian man sort of way, but she had not expected such blatant homophobia. She was too stunned to say anything and just shrugged it off saying, "Dad for the last time, he is not gay."

The less said the better, was her tactic with Dad. But she would always regret not addressing that homophobic and downright nasty remark with her father. Why hadn't she just told him that she had no problem with gay people and that love is love and it's a non-issue and the world is different now than when he grew up and gay people aren't 'bad' or any of the million other things she was thinking?

She thought all of this, but said nothing. And years later, she would come to regret it.

"She hasn't understood yet. She still thinks keeping quiet is the way to keep the peace," God observed.

"She still doesn't see her problems as learnings," The helper responded.

"Ughhh. . .Why else would we be giving them to her?"

"Many think it's because we are bored," The helper replied sheepishly, at which they both chuckled.

And just like that, G's frustration dissipated.

With billions of souls to guide through infinity, boredom wasn't a luxury they afforded. Neither was prolonged frustration.

***

On her return back to NYC, a week before Nadia's twenty third birthday, Chris came over. He had had a big, yell-till-the-neighbours-think-someone-is-getting-murdered kind of fight with Gabby. They had been *on again, off again, on again,* for the past year or so now.

"What was it about this time?" Nadia asked while they strolled along her street. She knew this would be an outdoorsy conversation; walking helped Chris think. So, in her PJs, at 2 am, despite the 9 am client presentation Nadia had the next day at work, she met Chris for a venting walk.

"That I didn't invite her to my cousin's wedding next week. She just doesn't get it, man! I'm not ready to be that public about it. We *just* got back together."

"But you have been on and off for a year or so. If it will make her happy, just take her no?"

"It's too soon. She needs to get that. I feel like we keep having a different version of the same fight over and over again."

"She wants something and you don't want to give it to her…yea it's a trend alright."

"I don't know what to do. I think I should just end it. For good this time."

Nadia didn't respond. 'For good' translated to 'till this problem blows over'. Chris had a way of evading issues with Gabby. Nadia knew it wasn't her place to say anything and so she held back.

"Why aren't you saying anything?" he asked after a few seconds of silence. He had been waiting for her response.

She just shrugged.

"What? Say it… what do you think?"

"But you don't want to hear it."

"I do! Tell me. What am I missing?"

"Chris! This is like the 300th time you and Gabby have had the same fight. And every time, you leave it unresolved. Make up sex when you get back together, isn't resolution enough. She is a nice girl. And she cares about you. Either cut her loose or frigging actually work on the relationship with her."

"Why are you yelling at me? What the fuck. I didn't come here for a lecture."

"Too bad! This is what I have to say. If you can't hear it from me, then…" Nadia exhaled as her body grew stiff with irritation over this repetitive drama.

She looked away and they continued walking for a minute in silence. Finally, she leaned in and gave Chris a sideways hug.

"Sorry for yelling. But I had to say it."

He allowed the hug but still said nothing. Then, after another minute, he began, "The lecture was right."

"I focus so much on all the good stuff with Gabby, and then just ignore the problems. I just want it to be… easy."

"Maybe it will be once you get through the shit. Like in *Shawshank Redemption*, when he escapes to that beach in Mexico, but first has to wade through, like miles of shit water in the sewage pipe."

"Wow. Great analogy. Thanks! Wait till I tell Gabby you compared our relationship to sewage."

"Shut up!" she said, swatting his head playfully.

That night after Chris went back home, Nadia thought about the continued Chris/Gabby saga and how it annoyed her, while lying in bed. It was on, then off, then kinda on, then definitely off, and then predictably on again. Always unaddressed. Unresolved.

Chris needs to break this pattern.

It was obvious to her. But not to Chris. Why?

And then… she realised!

If only I could see my own patterns this clearly.

She knew she had them, but they were hazy. Like looking through a frosted glass on a foggy day; you can see a shadowy outline, but aren't really sure who or what is forming it.

But then, it occurred to her – maybe her patterns, were obvious to Chris.

Could it be? Are we clearly visible to those close to us? Or are we the same sphinx that we see in the mirror.

Mirror! That's it! Is that the answer? Wow G. Is this your tactic? Could Chris help show me the patterns in myself that I can't see? Like a human mirror.

The helper closed his eyes; he could relax a little now. Once they want to learn, to grow, to see... they do!

G's human mirror tactic worked every time.

***

Three nights later, when Chris and Nadia met for a stroll through alphabet city, she decided to broach the subject with him.

"Chris… I have a question to ask you."

"What?"

"I've been thinking about patterns we all get stuck in, that we just can't see. You know what I mean?"

"Ummm not really."

"I mean like a mistake we keep repeating, because we are too 'in it' to notice. But an outsider can see it right away. Like how we all can see that Connie needs to be piss drunk every time she is around new people."

"Yea," Chris replied, still not sure where this was headed.

"But, the way we all see it, clear as day, Connie can't. Just like that, I probably have a pattern that I can't see. But maybe you do?" Nadia explained, glad to have finally expressed her thoughts clearly.

"Sooooo you want me to be your Shrink?" Chris asked coyly.

"NOOOO," Nadia exclaimed, but Chris cut her off.

"Listen, you better start paying me. I think I need remuneration. And dental benefits. I may have mouths to feed one day, you know!"

"Ufff! Actually, you should pay *me*! I have put up with so much of your whining over the years. And what about that business studies paper I helped you write in sophomore year."

"Damn! That was like four years ago. It's true what they say – an elephant never forgets!"

"Did you just call me an elephant?? I'm going to kill you! Hahahah. Okay now seriously... tell me- Is there any pattern you see, that I don't?"

After he was done chuckling, Chris went quiet for a couple of seconds. Nadia looked at him expectantly, waiting for his reply. She knew that whatever it was, she could take it, coming from Chris. He wasn't a critical person and would never say something just to be hurtful.

Slowly, Chris began "With you, I think your greatest strength, can also be your weakness."

"What do you mean?"

"Your ability to be independent. It's a great quality, but I think you take cover behind it sometimes. Like 'oh I don't need anyone. I'm fine on my own'. And yes you will be fine on your own. But you would be *better,* if you gave people a chance to help you. If you let people in."

"But I let you in," Nadia said, instantly realising how defensive she sounded.

"True that. But after almost a year of knowing me. Only then did you really start telling me anything of substance. It took you very long to trust even me. And I'm sure it comes from the way you grew up, but…"

Nadia exhaled and Chris stopped talking, probably noticing her changing demeanour.

"Have I upset you?" he asked cautiously.

"No… no. I think you're right. I use my independence almost like a shield sometimes. Truth is, I do need… and want people in my life."

"We all do."

"Yup."

"I'll try and work on that. It's just hard to be more open and trusting. I feel like if I open up, I'm making it easier to get hurt. Better not to expect stuff, you know."

"But if you don't open up, you're also losing out. You just don't know it."

"Yeah…yes you're right oh wise one. When did you become so sage?"

"I'm a man of many talents," Chris replied smugly.

"I'll keep that in mind oh wise one. Thanks!"

"Anytime, Bambi."

And with that, Nadia had been shown a pattern, that now she had to work on breaking. And she got a new nickname. After that, Chris only called her Bambi, and soon it caught on with all their friends.

**

'Happy Birthday Bambi' was the message on the cake that Connie baked for Nadia's twenty-third birthday. All of them met at their usual bar on 9th Street and 3rd Avenue. It wasn't fancy, it wasn't even very clean, but it was FUN. They played foosball and darts and a drinking game that made everyone do a shot every time someone walked in or out of the bar. Since it was a Friday night in New York City, it is safe to say that the foot traffic at the bar, got all of Nadia's friends very, very drunk.

After the bar, they moved the party back to Nadia's apartment. She now lived alone in a 3rd floor walk-up, studio apartment, on the Lower East Side. She had decided that twenty-three was too old to have roommates any more, and she needed her own space. So, she had found this place and moved in a month ago. The kitchen was a 4 foot long counter with a sink at the end, but at least she could now cook at all hours of the night, never worrying about disturbing her roommates. That night, the studio felt particularly puny with eleven people in it, but a little bit of cramping never hurt anyone. (except Connie's new boyfriend, Tyler, who tripped over someone's outstretched leg while he was trying to get to the bathroom)

They were all sitting on the floor in a large circle and had been playing 'Cards Against Humanity'.

"Oops! Now Tyler should be called Bambi too. Because he can barely walk," Nadia joked, the intoxication clear in her voice.

"By that logic, we are all Bambi tonight. Alcohol powered Bambi's!" Isla replied, making everyone laugh.

It was true. All of them had walked home like toddlers who had just learned to take their first few steps. And who better to point it out than Isla, who could have been a stand-up comic if she had wanted to. Sadly, she deprived the world of that pee inducing joy and instead was becoming a counsellor – Dr. Isla R. (PHD)

"Islllla you are the drunkest of usss all," Chris said, slurring his words.

"Umm I'm pretty sure that's you, hun," Gabby said, while turning to Chris to give him a sloppy peck on the cheek. To which everyone responded with a resounding "Awwww."

"Yeah Chris," Isla agreed, "But it's your bestie's birthday, so you are excused."

"Who? That one…?" Chris replied pointing to Nadia, who was across the room, sitting hand in hand with Connie, Nadia's work-wife.

"Her parents pay me to be her friend," Chris continued in a mock hushed tone.

"Oh my god. They pay you too," Isla replied, instantly playing along. "They also pay *me*."

"And me," Gabby yelled.

"And me," Connie said.

And one by one, everyone chimed in to say that they had been paid by Nadia's parents to be her friend as the room filled with high pitched, drunken giggles.

"Guyssss my parents aren't that rich! They couldn't afford to buy me ELEVEN friends. Maybe one or two…" Nadia replied, but she was drowned out by the chanting that had begun.

"Happy Birthday, Bambi. We want a raise. Happy Birthday, Bambi. We want a raise. Happy Birthday, Bambi. We want a raise," they all said like a well-trained, but drunk, choir.

Nadia nearly peed her panties from laughing too hard that night. After the cake had been cut and eaten, and everyone left, she went to bed exceptionally grateful for not one, not two, not three…but eleven unpaid, great, dependable friends.

G smiled at the intoxicated revelry.

"Happy Birthday, Nadia."

The helper had obliged. Happy it had been.

CHAPTER 6

THE STORM

That November, Chris and Nadia set out on their Thanksgiving break adventure.

They had been planning it for weeks with daily phone calls or texts to confirm the minutest details of this plan. This would be their last 'discover' of the year as Nadia was going back to Mumbai in December for a quick meet the family trip. She had planned the trip, after her talk with Chris about her pattern. She wanted to break it and was actively and consciously trying to let people in.

"You know I even reached out to Connie, Isla, Gabby and Tara this week. I called them all for a phone catch-up session. And I spoke about *my* life. I'm trying to open up some more."

"Good job, Bambi," he said mimicking a school teacher's encouraging tone.

"Okay, now dish! How was the wedding? Did Gabby enjoy?" she asked. Chris had finally agreed to take Gabby to his cousin's wedding and had even introduced her to his family. This was a BIG deal.

"It was better than I expected actually. It was nice to have her around. Everyone loved her."

"And do *you*?" Nadia asked coyly. She knew Chris loved Gabby, he just hadn't admitted it yet.

He didn't respond. Just smiled and kept his eyes on the Long Island Turnpike on their way to 'Caumsett State Park'.

She let it pass, for now. She would have plenty of time over the weekend to ask him again and again. She knew that he probably wasn't saying anything yet because they were headed for a two-day camping trip and if he started the trip by admitting he loved Gabby, Nadia would one million percent try and convince him to tell Gabby. He was probably baby stepping it.

They drove on, as it started to get dark. The sun was setting earlier and earlier as November neared its end. In fact, a freak snowstorm had been predicted by the weather channel for that night. But Chris and Nadia dismissed it. Who had ever heard of snow as early as the 26th of November! Surely the weather channel had gotten it wrong. This was New York, not Newfoundland.

But, by seven it started snowing (Weather channel – 1, Chris & Nadia – 0). It was pitch dark, snowing lightly, with no other cars around, and everything looked simply gorgeous in that secluded part of Northern Long Island. The snow was so light, that they didn't think to turn back or check into a motel for the night. Camping would be exciting in this weather, they decided. Besides, they were well equipped. The RV had heating and they had their all-weather boots on. What could go wrong?

They turned a corner, as the radio signal of the RV started to fluctuate. They had been listening to old rock music on the local radio station to set the 'camping mood', but now all they could hear was static. This happened on the North Shore sometimes, and a little fiddling around with the radio, usually did the trick. Chris stretched out his arm to adjust the radio knob, but the static sound continued.

His eyes were only averted for a second, but as soon as he looked back up at the road, he saw the fox. It was looking straight at them, frozen, dead-centre on the road, probably blinded by the headlights. Nadia saw it first and yelled "Look out!"

Chris immediately honked and swerved slightly to avoid hitting the fox, but he misjudged the grip of the tyres. The RV tyres couldn't handle the lack of traction caused by the snow and they careened off the road, picking up speed as they barrelled towards a patch of trees to the right. The road was almost a foot higher than the ground flanking it and the RV began to tilt to the right with the speed and force of the descent off the road. It all happened so fast. On impact, Nadia blacked out for a couple of seconds.

When she regained consciousness, she could taste blood in her mouth. She was hanging in her seat, fastened by the seatbelt, with the airbag in her face. It took her some time to realise that they had hit the trees and the RV had toppled onto its side. As she slowly turned her head left, to check on Chris, her blurry vision cleared and she realised with horror that his grey sweater had a large blood stain on its left side. The blood had oozed through multiple layers of clothing in a matter of maybe a minute, which meant…

But where is the blood coming from? She couldn't see a wound.

"Chris… Chris wake up. Where are you hurt?" she yelled, reaching out to try and shake him. She could barely reach him as she was immobilised by her seatbelt and the airbag. But luckily, he woke up, delirious.

His voice was strained and hoarse when he finally mumbled, "I don't know."

He weakly tried to move his neck to assess his body but he couldn't. He too was pinned down in the seat by the belt and airbag.

But by then, Nadia had spotted it – the branch that had impaled his left shoulder through the shattered window. It entered his shoulder from the front, but Nadia couldn't see all the way over Chris to gauge the extent of the wound. She could tell that he was in and out of consciousness, which was not a good sign.

"Chris, hang on okay. I'm calling 911. They are going to come and get us," she yelled, adrenaline taking over. She tried not to panic. She couldn't allow the fear to take over, she had to help Chris. Get them out of the RV. Get help. There was no time for anything else in that moment.

As she reached into her pocket for her phone, she couldn't find it. It had dropped to the floor during the crash. She had to get the damned seatbelt off!

She used all her strength to try and unlock the belt, frantically pushing and pulling at the clasp for what seemed like a long time, but it refused to budge. She couldn't move. Couldn't find her phone. Couldn't help Chris.

As this realisation set in, the tears welled up in her frightened eyes. Like a monsoon downpour, they began falling as she once again turned to Chris.

"Chris... does it hurt? Talk to me?"

By now, his entire sweater was soaked red. He wasn't talking, his eyes were barely open. The only sound Nadia could hear, over her own thumping heart, was his strained breathing; it was loud and laboured.

"Chris," she cried. But he didn't respond. "Christopher!!!" she screamed again, her voice shrill with panic. "Wake up, Chris. The police are on their way," she lied.

"Wake up. I need you to wake up."

But he didn't. He couldn't hear her.

And then she heard it as clear as an explosion.

She would never forget that sound. The sound of life fluttering away.

One second, his breathing was loud and wheezing, and the next it slowed down and then... nothing.

His breathing… stopped.

How easily he had slipped away. After that, she couldn't hear anything, not even her own heart or the engine whirring. It was as if she had gone deaf while the knowledge of what had happened, took over.

Chris has gone quiet. Chris isn't breathing anymore. Chris has stopped breathing. No breathing. No breath. No sound. No…

She stared mutely at his lifeless face, unable to look away. He looked the same as he had an hour ago except his eyes were shut. Chris was gone.

Nadia's world went quiet.

Then, the flashlight hit Nadia straight in the eyes, and roused her from her daze.

"Heyyy. Heyyy. Are you okay?? I've called 911. They are on their way. What's your name? Hey… girl? Are you okay?? You are going to be okay. You hear me…"

The man was kneeling outside the windscreen of the RV, yelling and waving his phones flashlight in Nadia's eyes to grab her attention. Nadia tore her gaze away from Chris and looked at the man, nodding weakly. She couldn't speak. She didn't want to speak. What was the point now? Chris was gone.

A minute or so later, she heard the sirens in the distance. They gradually grew louder and soon dozens of policemen, paramedics and fire fighters surrounded the

RV. They cut off the seatbelts and pulled Chris's body, and Nadia, out of the RV.

Nadia was being wheeled away as para medics tried to ask her questions.

But all she could see and hear was the attempt to resuscitate Chris. She saw them shock his chest thrice, as it jumped up each time and then, lay lifeless once again. Through all the movement, sirens, men and women in uniforms that surrounded her, Nadia's every sense was singularly focused on Chris's body. She prayed in her mind and willed him to move, to take one breath, to come back.

Breathe Chris. Come back... don't leave me. Please. Please G.

But until they closed her ambulance doors, he remained limp.

After that Nadia doesn't remember much. They sedated her and she woke up the next day in a hospital bed. The nurse informed her that her mom and dad were flying into NYC that night. They would be with her in the hospital tomorrow.

"What about Chris?" Nadia asked impatiently, with a remaining sliver of hope. "How is my friend? Is he... alive?" She had to know for sure. Maybe she imagined it all? Maybe Chris was okay. Maybe he had made it after all.

The nurse leaned in and touched Nadia's shoulder, "I'm sorry, honey," she said, concern and kindness all over her face. "He didn't make it. He was already gone when the ambulance got there. They couldn't revive him. I'm so sorry."

***

Nadia's parents stayed for two weeks and attended Chris's funeral with her. The funeral was unbearable. The pain in her heart must be what heart attacks feel like, except hers was slower and sustained. To see everyone who had known, loved and lost Chris, all gathered in one white rose-filled church, was emotionally overwhelming.

Nadia had to face his mother, father, sister, cousins, Gabby and all their friends. She had to see their pain, while feeling her own. Everyone was shattered. Everyone was confused and broken by the suddenness of the accident. Nobody had had a chance to say goodbye. Nobody could understand why this had happened.

Nadia had already repeated the heart wrenching details of that night to the police, doctors, Chris's mom and dad, her parents, Gabby and the hospital psychiatrist. They all wanted to know. They all wanted to talk about that night, over and over again. And all Nadia wanted to do was erase it.

She got though the funeral somehow as she slipped into auto-pilot, recalling her childhood tactic of shutting down to avoid the ouch feeling. Except this time, ouch didn't nearly describe it.

For five days after the funeral, all Nadia did was sleep. And had the same recurring dream – her phone is ringing, she looks at the screen and it says CHRIS. She answers immediately, hopeful, excited. Desperate to talk to him she yells, "Hello Chris? Where are you?" But there is no reply. She keeps shouting into the phone "Hello… Hello… Chris? You there?"

On waking up, Nadia would cry softly, and then fall asleep again. Mourning is exhausting business.

"Nadia, you must come back to India with us. You need to stop this," Mom said a week after the funeral. "Get yourself out of this funk… life goes on,"

Funk?

"Yes Mom, I know life goes on. Thanks," Nadia responded coldly. One week of grief was all she was allowed apparently.

"How will you even afford to stay here now? It doesn't seem like you will be able to go back to work. Just come home," Mom said while Dad, sat in the corner quietly. For the last week, he had gone about her studio apartment, tidying up and re-arranging everything over and over again, as if he wanted to glue it all in place. Nadia had noticed his attempts to make the room look perfect and had left him to it. That was his process, and avoiding both her parents was hers.

"I have savings," Nadia responded. She couldn't believe she was actually talking about money right now.

"Because your Dad said he can't afford to help you out monetarily. And you know I can't!"

That was essentially Mom's way of saying 'don't think of asking us for money. I checked with your Dad. It's a no from him. What a guy, right? I tried.'

Nadia was too exhausted to even be angry. She submitted. She knew what Roxanne was really trying to get at.

"Mom. Dad. I'm going back to work. I don't need your money. I'll be fine. You both can go home now. Thank you for coming here to help me."

"Oh, great decision. And you're most welcome, darling! You are our only daughter; of course we came. We thought you had been injured. Thank god you are fine," Mom said, choosing to not pick up on Nadia's robotic tone.

Physical injuries are the only ones that matter apparently. The only ones that required parental help to heal. And Nadia had none of those. All she lost in the accident was one tooth! And Chris.

"Good girl, Nadia. That is the right choice. Work will be an excellent distraction in fact," Dad said, walking over to her. He stroked her hair to show his approval. "Keeping busy always helps."

At least there was one thing Mom and Dad agreed upon!

***

So, a little over ten days after the accident, Nadia went back to work. Once they were sure Nadia was being 'productive' again, her parents went back to Mumbai too.

"Call us anytime, okay. Day or night," Akbar said as they got into a taxi headed for JFK.

Nadia nodded with an insincere smile.

"Bye, baby," Mom said, hugging Nadia goodbye, "You are such a strong girl. They are lucky to have you at eWay. Everything will be okay soon. Just stay busy." And with that they were off.

They were clearly confident that Nadia would be 'okay', probably thinking – 'Such is life, you know. People die. You have to just move forward. We have done our duty.'

In truth, Nadia was glad they'd left. Now she could grieve in peace. Her irritation and disappointment at their continued emotional incompetence had just added to the weight she had felt on her chest for the last two weeks.

She let out a sigh as their taxi pulled away. She walked back into her apartment building and headed straight for her couch. TV on. Volume up. Nadia off.

CHAPTER 7

TRYING TO MEND

So this is what high-functioning grief feels like.

Every thought hurt. Her forehead was actually physically sore from being permanently creased. She constantly wondered *why did this happen? What could have gone differently? I should have done something more. Why Chris and not me? Why am I still here and what am I supposed to do now? He left me… why, why, why?*

And beyond all the confusion and whys, lay the immeasurable sense of loss. You can't even call it emptiness, because to be empty, is to feel that space and know it isn't occupied, for now.

This was different – Nadia felt damaged. Like a parcel that had come in the mail and had been shattered by the rough handling of life; the packaging torn, stained and falling apart.

The parcel inside, broken to pieces, useless now.

And this feeling came with no hope. She was sure she would never feel better. She would never feel okay. She would never move past the day she looked over at Chris, as the life slipped from him. She would never forget the smell of the blood in the RV and his blood-stained grey sweater. How trapped and panicked she had felt then.

Just like she hadn't been able to move then, hadn't been able to save him, she wasn't able to move now. She wasn't able or willing to save herself.

She went to work, like a *good girl*. Said she was okay and getting better to anyone who asked, like a *good girl*. Didn't make people uncomfortable with her drama, like a *good girl*. She had easily relapsed into the old habit of not letting anyone in. *Good girls* are taught to not be too much to handle. She had decided that to be honest about the raw damage inside her, would be too much drama.

Nobody can understand. Nobody can help. And frankly, nobody wants to know the gory details.

So, she didn't talk about them. *Good girls*, like old habits, die hard.

But she went over the gory details every day in her mind, at work and after and before. Her body was on autopilot, while her mind was stuck on 26th November, and her heart was stuck in that whirlpool of pain. Her breath had felt strained for a month now, as if someone was sitting on her chest, all day, every day. Controlling her tears till night-time was no easy task, but she managed on most days.

So, this is what baggage feels like, eh, G! she thought one night, while weeping quietly in bed, her pillowcase drenched with salty heartache.

"At least she hasn' t lost her sense of humour, grey as it may be for now, " The helper remarked.

G said nothing. He was just glad she still spoke to him and didn' t view him as the enemy or pain-giver.

Chris had his own story and his own pre-decided time to exit the world. But most people blame G when they are in that much pain.

Nadia had decided that no amount of baggage could kill her love for G. That death at least, was in her control!

To Chris from Bambi: Exploring The Scar

Even though you have left me,
And the wound feels like it can never heal,
The scar tissue starts to grow.

Will the mark ever disappear?
I am almost afraid of fully mending,
For fear it will sever our connection.

I want to continue holding on to you.
The scab is my reminder,
So, I keep picking at it.

I know the smart thing to do:
Neosporin and leave it alone.
The scab will fall off eventually.

I have decided I must try.
I will put mittens on my heart,
And attempt goodbye.

***

Gabby and Nadia met for coffee one month after the accident. It was the day after Christmas and Gabby was in pretty bad shape. She had hoped this would have been her first holiday season with Chris, and she was consumed by her broken heart. Nadia knew she owed it to Chris to help Gabby feel better.

It was snowing outside, and so after coffee, they decided to take a walk. Nothing like a walk in the snow to discuss matters of a grieving heart.

They walked and walked and walked through Central Park North, past the Harlem Meer that was semi frozen now, through the Conservatory Gardens with all the bare trees and sans the tulips that light it up in the springtime. Finally, they sat down on a bench under a majestic but leafless elm tree, while the snow fell around them.

They spoke about Chris, his smile, how much he was missed, and how hard it was to know that he would never return. They would never sit with him or talk to him again.

Then, Nadia took Gabby's glove covered hand in hers and they sat there in silence, watching the snow fall and letting nature and friendship soothe them.

"Gabby, he loved you, you know," Nadia said. Gabby needed to know how Chris had truly felt about her, since he hadn't gotten a chance to tell her himself.

"He told you that?" Gabby asked.

"Yes. And he was going to tell you… but…"

They both knew how that sentence ends.

Gabby just looked at Nadia and then said, "Thank you."

Nadia didn't respond and after a minute of sitting in silence, she asked "How are you going to move on?"

"How are you?" Gabby asked back, after a couple of seconds. Nadia hadn't considered that step yet.

"With your help!" she responded, remembering the advice Chris had given her about asking for help.

"Deal, Bambi!" Gabby replied, breaking into a smile for the first time that day.

CHAPTER 8

SERENDIPITY AT THE END OF THE TUNNEL

A few weeks later, Gabby came over one evening and forced Nadia to set up a Hello Cupid account along with her. They were going to do this together, she said. They needed to feel better and no distraction could be easier (or funnier) than online dating!

Nadia meekly agreed. Maybe it wasn't the worst idea to try and date. And if it helped Gabby, she would play along. Baby steps.

Nadia couldn't believe her eyes when she woke up the next morning to find thirty-two notifications waiting for her on her phone.

I have thirty-two prospective matches…! WTF. How??

Some of the messages she received in the days to follow were ridiculously hilarious. She and Gabby would screenshot the funniest ones and send them to each other.

She couldn't deny how effective this actually was; she was being silly again. Laughing.

"Hi gorgeous. Wanna come over for a home cooked meal at my crib?" wrote Manofyourdreams86

"Wow you are the woman I've been waiting for" Wrote Dan_theman

"Hey girl. Looks like you could use a foot rub. And nobody rubs feet better than me," wrote Nicholast22

Cringe-worthy as they were, the messages Gabby received were even worse. Gabby was Dominican and to deny she looked like JLO would mean, you're blind. She was curvy, in all the right places, had thick long brown hair, brown eyes and a walk that could make anyone's head turn. And the men on 'Hello Cupid' noticed.

"Ola Mami. I want to kiss your caramel skin and give you my heart. When can we meet? I want to see if you are real or an angel sent from purrfectland," wrote Daddyeddielovestheladies

"Pinch me? I have never seen a more stunning woman. Really. Please meet me?" wrote Kevin_Ruscito

"Meet me at 9 tonight. Joshua Tree bar on 60th and 1st for the best date you will ever had," wrote DTF Jake

Nadia and Gabby were shaking with hysterical laughter after reading these. It was a cold wet February Sunday when they met at the IHOP in the village to swap Hello Cupid gossip. After reading all the laugh out loud messages the two of them had received in the past week, they went on to the three messages that seemed like they were written by real human beings living on planet earth.

Gabby had gotten two 'normal' messages. One from a hot architect named Max and one from a double bass player out in Jersey named Lukas.

And Nadia had gotten a message from a Parsi guy from Mumbai, who had moved to NYC two years ago – Zaal Irani. What were the odds!!! There are barely 60,000 Parsis (a small religion whose followers live mostly in India) left in the world, and Hello Cupid had connected her to one from Mumbai, who now lived ten blocks away from her!

"So are you going to meet this guy?" Gabby asked. "That's your religion right?"

"Yeah not that I'm religious at all but… I think I kinda have to meet him," Nadia admitted. It was just too serendipitous to not explore. Plus, his photo looked cute.

So, Gabby went on a date with the sexy musician from Jersey and Nadia met the cute investment banker from Mumbai.

***

On their first date, Zaal took Nadia to a little Cuban restaurant on the upper west side. The first thing Nadia noticed about him was his formal manner. He was an investment banker alright! He came to dinner in a grey business suit, shiny shoes, slick hair and an expensive watch. He spoke in complete sentences and said things like "Having said that…" and "Contrary to popular belief…" and "This wine is faintly reminiscent of…" It was like being in an episode of *Frasier* and *not* what Nadia was used to.

Physically too, Zaal was not what Nadia had expected. He was extremely muscular, but short. Just around 5'6, and seemed as tall as Nadia when they stood next to each other. He was twenty-eight, pale, clean shaven, had a very confident gait and the perfect Parsi nose- hooked and long. His face had definite character but he wasn't instantly attractive.

However, he had a sense of humour and spoke to Nadia in Gujarati! She hadn't realised how starved her ears had gotten for her sweet language. It was like a familiar melody and she couldn't help but sing along. There were also some very typically Mumbai things that they bonded over, like their shared love of soulful Bollywood music, discussing the intense heat and heavy rain and how homesick they both felt sometimes, despite loving NYC.

And while speaking of these things, Zaal became a different person, less corporate, more real. He got a glint in his small dark eyes that crinkled at the sides when he smiled, while talking about his college days in Mumbai. Even his body language changed when he spoke of home. It was as if there were two Zaals living in one, buff (I-hit-the-gym-every-single-day) body; Mumbai Zaal and Corporate Zaal.

Corporate Zaal spoke about his work, his long hours, the articles he had read about BREXIT and the impact of ISIS on global market trends. Mumbai Zaal spoke about his home, his mother and his fun college days. Mumbai Zaal asked Nadia questions. Corporate Zaal spoke and spoke and spoke.

After dinner, as he walked Nadia to the subway, he reached for her hand. Nadia hadn't expected it because in her experience, Indian men were usually a little gun-shy at first. As soon as he did it though, Nadia noticed how nice it felt. And once they reached the subway entrance, he turned to face her, gently wrapped his free hand around her lower back and came in for a kiss. No hesitation. Smooth as silk.

He was a gooood kisser. So good that he left Nadia blushing as their lips parted and eyes met.

"Umm…" Nadia said, unable to form a sentence.

"You free next Friday?" he asked.

"Ummm… yeah. You have something in mind?" Nadia muttered, still a little zapped.

"I have a Valentine's Day office party to attend. Come with me? It may be boring though."

"Umm. Sure. I'll come with you."

"Great. I'll text you. I had a great time tonight, Nadia," he said, turning around to walk away.

"Yea me too. Bye."

"Goodnight. Get home safe." And with that he was off. Nadia entered the subway and tried to compose herself. She didn't know what to make of this guy.

She reached home, got into bed and then waited for her gut to speak to her… "What's Zaal about?" she asked her gut. "Do I like him?"

Yes, she did. There was something about him; sort of like a déjà vu feeling. She could tell that he was full of himself and he had done most of the talking that night, but there was something about him. Also, that night, after a long time, Nadia fell asleep 'un-sad'.

Even pre- Reset, Zaal had helped Nadia through this phase of her life.

"I just hope she doesn't make the same mistake as last time," The helper said. G said nothing. They would have to let this one play out. Wait and watch.

The following Friday night they went for his office Val day party, where she saw more and more of Corporate Zaal. His voice was louder, like he wanted to be heard. His posture was straighter, like he wanted to be seen. He held Nadia's waist, got her drinks and was extremely attentive, but it just seemed a little... put on. He didn't seem natural. It was a little bit like being out with a date-robot. He did all the right things, but she wasn't sure if it was because he *felt* like doing them. It was turning Nadia off but then... he got drunk.

With every glass of whiskey that he drank, more and more of Mumbai Zaal got infused into his personality, and Nadia too began to ease up around him. They laughed while discussing an old Indian horror TV show they both used to watch as children – *Zee Horror*, and how ridiculous the plot of every episode now seemed to them. At 1 am they left the party and walked hand in hand to a bar at the end of the block. There, they moved onto shots and Zaal even took off his tie and jacket, and rolled up his sleeves!

"You have gorgeous eyes, you know," Zaal said to her after their third shot.

"Oh thank you!" Nadia responded with a mock flutter of her eyelashes. She was too drunk to feel inhibited anymore.

"I'm serious! They are very pretty."

"And you are a very good kisser," she replied with a mischievous smile and her best come hither look. Clearly, she was now drunk enough to flirt.

Zaal didn't need any more hints. He smiled, clearly pleased by the compliment, leaned over to her bar stool and kissed her, gently at first and then with more and more passion. Nadia responded by placing her hand on his thigh and running her other hand over the back of his neck and into his hair. Even drunk, his kissing skills did not disappoint.

After about a minute of this, he broke away from her lips and said, "Come back to my place? I live two blocks from here."

Usually, Nadia would have said no. It was only their second date; way too soon for her. She hardly knew the guy. But, she hadn't felt this 'un-sad' in months now. She hadn't felt twenty-three in months now. The alcohol, the laughing, and of course, the extremely sexy kissing, had made Nadia feel light again. So, she went with it.

"Umm. Yea let's do that," she replied, already putting on her coat that had been sitting in her lap. Zaal instantly gave his credit card to the bartender and in a minute, they were out of there.

Still buzzed, they held each other's waist and walked the two short blocks to his fancy apartment building, where the doorman smiled a knowing smile at Zaal, when they walked in. Clearly this wasn't uncommon for Mr Smooth. That didn't bother Nadia one bit though. In fact, it made her more certain that the night would be fun. And it was!

They started making out on the elevator itself, and once in the apartment, they moved very quickly to his bedroom. Zaal unbuttoned his own shirt and took off his pants, while still kissing Nadia's neck and then stood back, while she undressed. He wanted the view, and as their eyes took each other in, they moved to meet each other again and let their hands take over. Skin on skin, all their senses completely focussed on each other.

The sex was urgent, passionate and smooth – the man knew what he was doing.

And after, when Nadia said she would head back home, he said, "Stay the night. It's late..." as he pulled her into bed once again. They fell asleep under his soft Egyptian cotton bedsheets.

The next morning, Nadia woke up and... grinned. There was no buyer's remorse. She felt totally satisfied.

Zaal was still sleeping, so she got up quietly to use the bathroom. He heard her though, and woke up.

As soon as he saw her, he smiled. It wasn't a 'I have a girl in my bed, yay for me' smile. It was a genuine smile, like he was happy to see her.

"You hungry?" were the first words out of his mouth.

"Actually yes. And a little hungover," Nadia replied realising that her tummy was queasy from all the drinking last night.

"I'll make you some Chai," he said getting out of bed. No sweeter words have ever been uttered. Chai! Not coffee. Not green tea. Not a chai tea latte. Just Chai!

Chai=home, and it made Nadia instantly beam from ear to ear. "Perfect! Thank you," she replied as he left the room to go to the kitchen.

Hmmm… for sure no regrets.

By the time she got dressed and went to the living room, Zaal had already made the chai and was sipping from a mug, while reading the news on his phone in an armchair by the floor to ceiling windows that overlooked the Manhattan skyline. Nadia grabbed the mug of chai he had left on the counter for her and sat down in the other armchair next to him.

"What a view!" she said, truly awed by its majesty. The only thing she could see from the two windows in her studio apartment, was the building across the street from her. She could look right into the opposite third floor apartment where two skinny college kids lived. They sat on their fire escape and smoked pot twenty hours a day, so Nadia's curtains had to remain drawn most of the time.

"Yea it's perfect for days like this. I love to just sit here with a cup of chai and think," Zaal replied. He seemed calm, relaxed. She was starting to like *this* Zaal. Also, he looked very cute reading the paper in his boxers. So much better than a suit and tie.

Just as she was admiring the view of Zaal and the skyline beyond, he asked, "What plans for today?"

"Oh, I usually do laundry on Saturdays. Nothing major. Maybe grocery shopping," Nadia replied, not understanding why he was asking. She thought he was just making chit chat because after six years, Nadia had gotten used to the American style of dating, where you NEVER spend the day with someone you have only gone on two dates with. Even if you've slept with them.

But, it seemed Zaal was still operating by Indian dating standards where if you want to get to know someone, you spend time with them, possibly the whole day, even if it's just after two dates and one night of yummy sex.

Since Nadia didn't go on, he asked again, "So you're not meeting anyone? You're free?"

That's when she understood. "Oh! Yeah, I'm free. Umm… Do you want to come with me?" she asked, tentatively.

"Sure!" he instantly replied, which puzzled Nadia. He wanted to spend his Saturday with her, to accompany her on her chores, after just two dates. Why?

Zaal got dressed as quick as a bullet train and off they went. He hailed a cab as soon as they got out of his building, even though Nadia's apartment was just ten blocks away! He didn't walk much, use the subway or the bus, she later found out. They spent the whole day together. He came with her to the laundromat across the street, to the grocery store, to Walgreens, kissed her, held her hand, they had sex once again and by 5 pm, Nadia wished he would leave.

She had had a fun day, and she liked the affection, and the orgasms, but this was too much. What happened to baby steps?

Not wanting to hurt his feelings, she said she had dinner plans with a friend. He said he too had to go to the gym and he would call her. Then he kissed her goodbye at her apartment door and left.

"Am I in the twilight zone?" Nadia asked Gabby, whom she had called as soon as Zaal left. "He spent the whole day with me. Who does that? After just one night?"

Gabby found it hilarious! "Girl, you found the one non-commitment-phobic guy in all of New York City."

"But... But we have only been on two dates. Now three I guess, if you count today."

"Bambi, I have a serious question to ask you," Gabby continued, in a teasing voice "How good are you? Cause clearly the sex blew his mind, if he didn't leave your side the entire next day."

"Honestly, he blew *my* mind. But I wasn't too bad either," Nadia joked, "that must be it."

But later that night, once she thought about it more, Nadia realised something. Zaal had only been in NYC two years. He hadn't gone to school here and probably didn't have too many friends yet, outside of work. And he had said, more than once, that he often felt homesick. So maybe he was lonely and connection starved, as so many people become when they live away from their homes. Maybe Nadia reminded him of home. Just like he did for her.

***

Two months into dating Zaal, Nadia still hadn't told him about Chris. She had barely even opened up to him about her challenging relationship with her parents yet. She was afraid to reveal her baggage to Zaal, as if it would make the relationship too… heavy. Also, she hadn't truly let Zaal in yet. Although she was consciously working on it.

Zaal had made Nadia meet his mother just five weeks into dating, when she visited him in NYC. It had scared Nadia immensely, but she was also flattered that he had considered her 'take home to Mum' material. His mother had been sweet and warm, and it was clear that Zaal was her sun, moon, stars, grass, ocean, rain… everything.

Zaal and his mother were very close and now his mother texted Nadia from Mumbai on a weekly basis to check in on her. And to ask about Zaal as well, of course. Nadia promised herself to tell Zaal about Chris before the end of their second month together.

When she finally told Zaal about the accident and how she had lost her best friend just two and a half months before they met, he seemed relieved. He looked at her, let out a sigh and said he had always felt something was weighing on her, and now he knew what.

"That must be so painful for you. We don't have to talk about it, if you don't want to, okay baby."

Nadia immediately nodded 'yes', for the act of just having this conversation had drained her and she didn't want to open the wound further at that moment. She figured, she would tell Zaal more the next time he asked. It would be nice to talk to someone about Chris in fact; to remember him aloud.

But Zaal never brought up Chris or the accident again.

At first, it was a relief to Nadia that Zaal didn't broach the subject again, because she convinced herself that maybe talking about what a loving, fun, dependable, deep friendship Chris and she had shared, would have been difficult for her. And it may make Zaal insecure too. It felt safer to have Chris almost become like a secret she didn't talk about with anyone, ever. He lived in her heart and mind, unshared by the world.

Isn't it better this way? How is the past relevant to Zaal and my now anyways.

And Zaal was okay leaving it that way. He didn't ask too many questions or discuss his past too much either. He always said he wanted to 'look forward'.

"Wallowing in the past just isn't my style, Nadia," Zaal said time and time again.

At that point, Nadia didn't see Zaal's pattern yet. But she would slowly begin to.

She started noticing how Zaal never spoke about his pain (if he had any), the death of his father, any ex-girlfriends, sad memories, nothing! And weirder than that, he would never carry on a conversation about any emotional or heart-related topic with Nadia, even when she brought it up.

It was almost as if Zaal didn't have the ability, or the will, to deal with things that required an Emotional Quotient. His conversation preferences stayed in the zone of their day to day lives, work, his future plans and of course politics. All brain, no heart.

Nadia began to need to talk about her past pain with Zaal, but after being shut down four separate times by him, she felt guilty bringing up any of it with him again. Maybe it was unfair to expect Zaal to listen to her troubles. And apart from this, Zaal said and did all the right things.

He called her every day, they went on dates every weekend, he had introduced her to his mom, bought her gifts and had even started to speak of a future with her. He told her 'I love you' three months into dating her and seemed to genuinely like her. All of this had made Nadia fall in love with Zaal.

He wasn't sentimental, but he was accessible. And maybe that was enough?

Maybe he will change in time, right G? Nadia wondered one night.

"If only true vulnerability was everyone's cup of chai," G remarked as Nadia drifted off to sleep.

CHAPTER 9

YIKES

Over the next year Nadia got more accustomed to Zaal. Nadia's friends liked Zaal, and they all hung out together several nights a week after work. Connie thought he was the perfect man – committed, intelligent, good in bed, supportive of her long hours at work, successful and all in all, marriage material.

Zaal, too, was opening up a little more around their friends and seemed… happier. He now talked less about work and 'the market', after Isla had incessantly mocked the way he spoke, likening it to the 'Agent Smith' character from 'The Matrix'. Nadia had found this comparison hilarious and completely spot on! She could easily picture Zaal saying, "Hello Mr. Anderson" with sunglasses on and an expressionless face.

By June, right before Nadia and Zaal were taking off on their first trip together, Nadia decided to probe Zaal further on his past relationships. She still knew nothing about Zaal's dating history.

After asking Zaal three separate times, he got an extremely irritated look on his face. The kind he always got when he had a boundary he didn't want crossed. Nadia would usually give in at this point, like the time he used 'the look' when Nadia had wanted to go for a girls spa weekend, the same weekend that Zaal had wanted to take her to his office Easter party. Or when Nadia had told Zaal she didn't like one of his office buddies who gave her the creeps, and she didn't want to hang out with him anymore. The irritated look usually did the trick, and Nadia would give in.

But this time, Nadia had prepared for the look and she tried to ignore it, and ploughed ahead.

"Zaal, I love you and I just want to know a little about your past. I promise you, nothing you tell me matters now. It's all in the past. I just want to *know*."

When he still didn't reply, she said "Once you tell me, we never need to discuss it again."

This seemed to turn something inside Zaal, who loved to 'look forward' and he submitted.

He began to tell Nadia about Riya, his ex.

"We dated for a long time," he began, "She was very sweet, but we were just in different places in our life. Finally I had to break it off."

Okay so far so good. That happens.

"I had no other choice. My transfer to New York came through and I knew long distance doesn't work."

"So you guys broke up before you moved here?"

"A little after. There would have been lots of drama if I had told her while I was in Mumbai. So I waited till I got here. Just easier that way you know."

"So how did you do it? Was she visiting you when you told her?" Nadia enquired, with a sinking feeling in her stomach.

"No. I called her up and told her. I had made up my mind and there was really nothing we could've done. Long distance doesn't work."

"How did she take it?" Nadia asked.

"Okay…I think. I haven't heard from her again. She didn't even return the ring, but frankly I don't mind that."

"Ring?"

"Yeah it was a gift. So why would I want it back, you know. But some men want the ring back."

How magnanimous he was!

"Wait wait. What are you saying? Were you and Riya…engaged?" Nadia felt the breath get caught in her throat as she connected the dots.

"Yes. When I proposed to her, I thought I would remain in India. Then, luckily, my transfer came through. You know how difficult these work-visas are. More often than not, you don't get the visa."

"You were engaged?"

That's a BIG detail he has just never spoken about.

"Is that bothering you?" Zaal asked, now a little quieter. He came over to Nadia and held her, trying to comfort her, but totally misunderstanding why she was upset.

"I only love *you* now. She is history," he said. He was so oblivious that he thought Nadia was jealous. Nadia wasn't jealous, she was horrified. Horrified that her boyfriend of one year could have discarded his fiancé so easily, for his job, and then never even mention it.

"How long were you both together?" Nadia asked, hoping that his answer would explain his lack of emotion.

Maybe it was just a quick fling-like romance. These things happen ya. Maybe that's why it ended so abruptly.

"Six years," Zaal replied, nonchalantly. "Since I was Twenty."

***

Nadia didn't sleep much that night. She knew she had promised Zaal that 'nothing he told her mattered now' and 'It was all in the past' but she was Horrified with a capital H, by his callous attitude.

Nadia wanted him to be able to trust her and to open up to her, so she tried not to judge Zaal for the way he had handled his break up, but there was no doubt about it- To Nadia, it was a big fucking deal, and she was Mortified! With a capital M; small letters just couldn't capture the emotion, you know.

She couldn't help but think what this new information said about Zaal. What it meant about Zaal's heart. Or lack thereof.

How could he be so selfish and unfeeling?

So, New York City and the corporate life hadn't made Zaal into a robot, he had had those 'leanings' even before he arrived.

Yikes! With a capital Y.

***

Three weeks later, Nadia and Zaal left for their long awaited vacation together. Zaal had planned the whole thing – where they would go, where they would stay, which beaches they would visit. They both only had a week off work and were determined to make it count. Nadia had gotten even this one week off after begging her boss repeatedly over the last month. Finally, Tom had relented and granted her this much needed break. Her first, after the ten days she had taken off after the accident.

Zaal wanted to go somewhere tropical and didn't want the hassle of applying for visas which is the bane of every Indian passport holder's existence. Therefore, he zeroed in on the US Virgin Island of St. Thomas.

Nothing like the aquamarine waters of the Caribbean Sea, to take your mind off a crazy few months at work and the Horror (with a capital H) of finding out that your boyfriend was dull in the Emotional Quotient department.

But the trip seemed just like what they needed; Zaal and Nadia were having a superb time. They spent every day by their hotel's cliff-perched infinity pool, watching the cruise ships go in and out of the St. Thomas bay, and lounging on some of the best white sand beaches in the world, with plenty of lovemaking every morning and night. All this meant that Nadia began to get over her mortification, little by little. Now it was a small m, not capital.

And who am I to judge Zaal anyways!

She too had had her fair share of messy breakups. Although, Zaal was her first long term boyfriend. They had been together almost a year and a half now. Which is why Nadia decided to cut Zaal some slack! So what if his work, and himself, were his top two priorities. His mum and Nadia were a solid third and fourth on the list, right? How could she expect more?

Besides, he may change over the years.

"She always hoped Zaal would eventually change," The helper commented, remembering Nadia' s pattern from before her Reset.

G just looked on silently. Would she make the right choice this time?

***

On their last day in St. Thomas, Nadia and Zaal went to spend yet another day at 'Magens Bay Beach'. It was just too perfect a place to not re-visit. The beach had white sand that was so soft to lie in, that you didn't even need a beach towel. And the water was calm, warm and glowed with the sunlight it reflected. It was clear to the point that you could see tropical fish swimming in it, while sitting on the beach! They chose a shaded spot on the far end of the beach, where it was quiet and you got a panoramic view of the whole bay and the green hills that surrounded it, like a verdant crescent moon.

They had been having such a carefree time on this trip and Nadia realised why – Zaal hadn't spoken about work at all in almost three days now. It was a pleasant, albeit surprising change.

"I love you, baby," Nadia said looking over at Zaal in that perfect 'this is what love stories are made of' moment.

He smiled while sipping his beer. "I love you too."

"I'm having the best time. Are you?"

"Yes babe. This has been a great trip."

"You know something," Nadia said, "the best part for me has been having you all to myself this past week. It feels like we have left life behind and can just enjoy. No jobs, no stress, no using our brains," Nadia joked, reaching over to hold Zaal's hand.

"Yea I know what you mean. But tomorrow back to the real world," Zaal said with a sigh, while taking her hand.

"Can I tell you something?" Nadia asked, realising that if just a tinsy change could help so much, it was worth a try!

"What?"

"I have a request to make. But I don't know how to say it."

"Tell me," said Zaal, curious now.

"I want us to talk a little less about 'work' once we get back to NYC. I know it's very important to you and I'm here to talk about your day and all…But I want us to talk more about other things as well… Can we try that when we get back please?" Nadia said trying to make it sound casual, although she had gotten nervous voicing this request.

"Sure we can," he responded immediately, "but I didn't know you felt this way. Can you tell me why?"

"So…" Nadia began after a second's thought, "I'm just not a fan of work-talk. My job is important to me too, and you know how stressful it gets. So I like to leave it behind at the end of the work day and think of other things… I think it also goes back to when I was young," She explained, "My Mom and Dad would come home every evening and for the most part, speak only about their work, how stressful it was, how annoying their respective bosses were, etc. etc. and I just think that if you and I left work behind a little bit, we could explore so many other parts of each other."

"But we do! We talk a lot. And you know, my job… my work is *extremely* important to me."

Nadia took a second to compose her thoughts and then replied, slowly:

"I get that, baby. Don't get me wrong. But sometimes, because of the amount we talk about work… I feel like you're my colleague or I am your mentee. I feel like we are always talking about your job, or mine. And then *if* there is time, other stuff. Can't we strike a balance? Talk more about the 'heart' stuff."

"Hahah heart stuff? You are too cute. Nadia I'm almost thirty now. We aren't in college anymore. This is real life, not a romance novel. This is what grown-ups talk about," he said with a cutting half smile.

OUCH!

The sad part was – Zaal really believed that.

Grown up=obsessed with your job

Immature=not obsessed with your job

Balance=what's that?

Robot-Zaal's remark pinched Nadia in a spot, deep inside. She was trying to ask for something important to her, but she had been met with condescension, and had been ridiculed for not being like Zaal – 'grown-up'. And it felt like he had said it on purpose! Zaal had a way of deliberately saying something harsh to shut a conversation down at times. He knew by now what pinched and would shut Nadia up.

When Zaal felt attacked, he would sting! And the sting did its damage – silent and deep.

"Just thought I'd let you know how I feel," Nadia said, recoiling into her shell now, as Zaal had known she would. Conversation over.

Zaal went on sipping his beer and enjoying his day. He concluded by saying "I will try, if that's how you feel." But he never did.

Duhhh!

Like always, Zaal said the 'right' thing, like a business appeasement strategy, that he had no intention of carrying out. Why compromise, when you can win?

Zaal's remark stung Nadia for days though. But she didn't have the guts to address it with him or ask him once again to balance his needs, with hers.

Eventually, she decided to let it go. *It was just one remark*, she told herself. *I'm probably over-reacting*, she told herself.

Maybe I should try being more accommodating of Zaal's needs, she told herself. *He is a great boyfriend. He loves me.*

And so, I can let it go when he occasionally hurts me.

Nadia didn't fight for her needs with Zaal that day, and it cost them both. Silence was the poison she didn't notice. It infected her love for Zaal with resentment and apathy.

"You got to go through the problems, Nadia, not around them," G said, knowing she couldn't hear him over the roar of life.

This was exactly the same mistake she had started out with the last time with Zaal too.

"But I feel that this time she will learn this lesson..." The helper said, trying to reassure G.

So they held tight, as her twenty sixth birthday approached.

CHAPTER 10

DOUBT MEANS DON'T

The conveyor belt kept moving and the next stop seemed to be a big, obese Indian wedding. After twenty five, the parents of most Indian girls begin hounding them to 'settle down' as they call it. Her parents were no exception in this one regard and they, along with Zaal ,were pressuring Nadia already. It had been nearly three years with Zaal now and 'settling down' was an imminent must.

But something had kept her away from agreeing to marriage, so far. First, it had felt like a little hum. It seized her like a gentle panic every time she thought of having children with Zaal.

He just isn't good with kids.

And she hoped that maybe his EQ would develop over time, but she wasn't sure. The doubt she felt was too strong. "Doubt means don't," she had heard Oprah say, and if there was ever a time to use that snippet of advice from Goddess O, this would be it.

So she didn't entertain the subject of marriage, in fact, she worked at avoiding it like a potent STD.

Every time Zaal discussed marriage or his future plans, which included her, she would make up a reason to fight with him. Unconsciously at first, and then very deliberately. This became their pattern and Zaal began to notice.

"Do you *ever* want to marry me?" he asked one day.

"Baby, I'm too young. I haven't even thought about marriage yet. There is so much I want to accomplish first. We are not ready."

"We, or you? Because I'm ready. I want to marry you, Nadia. I'm going to love you forever and I want to start a family with you one day. What's the problem?"

How could she tell him that the problem was that she wasn't sure if he was THE ONE? How could she tell him that she couldn't imagine raising children with him. How could she tell him that she was scared of repeating her parent's mistakes?

So instead, she just said, "I want to establish my career first. You know how busy work keeps me. Where do I have the time or energy to think about marriage right now, baby?" She hoped that such a Zaal-like response would be easy for him to accept and would buy her at least a year or two. And even more than that, she desperately hoped, that by then she would *want* to marry Zaal.

God sighed. "Why won't she use her courage? Why won't she choose to be happy?" But he already knew the answer to that.

The helper suggested, "Shall we give her another sign?"

"Can' t hurt right?"

And so they did.

***

She was twelve days late. Her period had always been super regular, and almost two weeks was tooooooo long a delay. The anxiety slowly grew from innocuous at first, to bordering on a full blown panic attack. Finally on day thirteen, she decided to get a pregnancy test. She and Isla got the test and five drops of pee and three minutes later, they were ready to find out what destiny had in store for Nadia.

The thirteen days leading up to the test had been agonising, for many reasons. First, Nadia did not ever want to find out whether she had it in her to get an abortion.

Second, she did not want her life to be derailed by one stupid oversight – they had had post-fight, unprotected sex *once* last month.

And third, somehow, she did not want to involve Zaal in this decision. The idea of telling him she could be pregnant seemed like the most frightening part of it all. Not that he would blame her or be angry, but because he would want to keep the child and get married, and it would be the 'right' thing to do.

Telling him would mean she would be trapped! Trapped at twenty six. Trapped with him. Raising a child with a man who had a low EQ. All in the name of 'right'.

***

Isla saw the pee stick first.

Then, for some reason, Isla hid the pee stick behind her back. What was going on? "Tell me… I can't wait another second. Am I safe?" Nadia practically jumped towards Isla, trying to wrench the answer from her. But Isla, silently moved a step back.

"What the F**k, Isla! What does it say?" Nadia demanded, her voice panicked, with a tinge of anger. This was no time to be messing around, and she had thought that Isla full-well understood the delicate situation at hand.

"I'll tell you in a minute. But first tell me something. What do you wish it says?

"Not pregnant obviously. I'm twenty six!" She yelled out.

"Okay. Understandable. But is being twenty six the *only* reason on your mind?" Isla had a look in her eyes. Like she was willing Nadia to reveal something deeper. Like she knew the answer, but wanted to hear Nadia say it.

"Huh? What are you talking about? Don't psycho-analyse me right now. This isn't the time." Nadia had never been this pissed at Isla, but Isla seemed unphased.

"Just give me an honest answer Nadia!" Isla held her gaze, firm and unflinching.

"Why are you doing this right *now*?" Nadia's voice got more high pitched with very second. She couldn't understand what was going on. Isla had never behaved this inconsiderate before. She needed her friend's support right, NOT an interrogation.

After almost ten seconds of holding each other's gaze in a stand-off that would have appeared ridiculously comical to anyone who were to walk into that bathroom to witness it, Isla asked again.

"What is the real reason you are so freaked out?"

Nadia blinked and realised she was holding her breath. She felt hedged in by Isla and this line of questioning. The answer was on her tongue, but should she say it out loud? She had never admitted it before. Not even to herself.

"Okay fine! F**k! I don't think Zaal's the one okay. Are you happy now?"

Nadia huffed as she covered her face with her hands, the pregnancy test momentarily forgotten.

Isla didn't say anything. She just stood there and let Nadia have her mini melt down. Now the words began to spew out and Nadia sank to the bathroom floor. Her tears almost catapulted out of her eyes even though she kept her face hidden by her palms.

"I don't think we are right for each other. I don't know what to do…." She sputtered between sobs.

"I just don't know what to do. I'm so fu***d up."

"What do you want to do?" Isla asked, calmly, as she sat down to be with Nadia, her hand stroking Nadia's hair as she looked down and continued her sob fest.

"I want…. I don't know." "I just… I just"

"I just don't want to end up like my parents!"

It had just come out. Nadia hadn't even thought it, but it had slipped out like subconscious word vomit – honest and stealthy.

In that moment, once again, Nadia became free of her illusions. She knew what she had to do. She looked up at Isla, the sobs dying down.

"I don't want to end up like my parents."

Isla looked into her eyes and understood. She could see her fear and heartache. She could see Nadia's mind churning now.

"I know what I need to do."

Isla nodded and hugged her tight as they sat there for a minute, the emotional whirlwind subsiding.

"You're kinda evil, you know," Nadia said, while her head rested on Isla's shoulder.

"I know," Isla replied, as they both smiled.

"I love it."

And with that, Isla handed Nadia the pregnancy test.

Nadia felt a weird sense of déjà vu in her belly the moment she looked at it. Had she been in this exact same moment before? How could this feel so... familiar?

The déjà vu, quickly gave way to relief. Nadia was not pregnant. Still safe. Still free.

"Last time, she had already succumbed to the pressure and was engaged to Zaal by the time this pregnancy test incident came around," G recalled.

And they both knew how that had ended up.....

"You think Nadia will act on her gut feeling this time?" The helper asked, knowing G didn't know either. They just had to let her choices in this Reset, unfold.

Oh free will! The bane/pain of the divine world.

***

After Isla left the apartment, Nadia sat down and took stock of her eventful evening. She now understood that it wasn't enough that her gut spoke to her when Zaal was around. Yes, he meant a lot to her. Yes, having him in her life these last three years had been lovely. Yes, she had grown tremendously with him. Yes, he had always felt oddly familiar. But also, Zaal was unemotional, work obsessed and averse to change or compromise. She knew what she wanted to do now. But could she do it?

115

That night, when Zaal came over to her place after the gym, she sat him down on the couch, looked into his questioning eyes and spat it out – "Zaal, this is very difficult for me to say…I…I want to end it. Break up. I'm so so sorry." They were the most heart wrenching words she had ever said in her life. She felt like a villain, a cruel man-eater.

Zaal's face dropped as if that was the last thing he had expected to hear. His face seemed almost cartoon like when his eyes filled with instant fury, and he spat out "WHAAT? Is this a joke?"

"You want to end it!!" he yelled at the top of his lungs, "Where is this coming from? Everything is going so well… Why? Tell me why?" he had stood up now and was waving his arms around in anger while he spoke. His heart and ego, both, had been attacked.

"Zaal, calm down. Let's talk about this calmly please," Nadia begged, a little taken aback, even though she had expected the anger.

"Oh you want me to be calm? You suddenly, after three years, tell me you want to break up? How can I be f*****g calm?"

Suddenly he seemed unhinged, "Have you found someone else? Had enough of me? Who is he?"

"Nooo…It's nothing like that," Nadia exclaimed, hurt by the accusation. "I love you. But… but…"

"This is how you show your love? But what…" Nadia hadn't expected this level of screaming. She didn't know his voice could get this loud.

She tried to maintain some composure and respond, but it was getting harder.

"But… it doesn't feel right, Zaal. I don't want to marry you and I don't want to lead you on anymore. You deserve better, I'm sorry. I really am," she said with tears filling up in her eyes now.

She knew how betrayed and angry Zaal was feeling. However, she knew that it was the right thing to do. Right, in the real sense of the word. She had to break his heart now, to avoid a true catastrophe later, for both of them. He wasn't THE ONE.

"You're sorry? Grow up, Nadia! You are throwing me away and you will sure as hell regret it. Nobody will give you all the things I can. You won't find someone better than me and then you'll regret this. Then don't come crying to me." With that, Zaal stormed out of her apartment, slamming the door behind him.

Nadia cried most of the night, feeling the guilt, loss and hurt that came with leaving a man she loved, and knew loved her, in his own way. But she didn't regret doing it; she had been true to herself.

The next day on her way back from work, Nadia bought herself a single, splendid red rose, to remind herself of love and beauty. Then she cooked herself a lovely chicken curry, barely ate any of it, and went to sleep early.

"Now the courage has kicked in," God said triumphantly.

The helper could hear the pride in his voice.

They had been waiting for this moment like die-hard fans waits to see the new season of their favourite Netflix show.

This was where she had faltered the last time! She hadn't heeded the signs. She hadn't left Zaal.

"It's always the 'almost perfects' that are most difficult to figure out," G remarked.

They had seen it through eternity, with billions of souls. And in her first life, before the Reset, Nadia had submitted to the 'almost' – Zaal, marrying him. A mistake that had led her down a different path.

The helper and G had watched her stumble through that life, making mistake upon mistake until finally she hit rock bottom! They could still remember the last day of Nadia's first chance.

On that last day of that life, she had been sitting in her bedroom, staring deep into the mirror, into her own dewy eyes, entranced by the flood of regret.

At seventy six, she had found out that morning that she had a rare form of Leukaemia. It had reached an advanced stage and the doctors gave her a few months to live. She was almost broke, had no insurance, and was aching all over from arthritis. She was utterly alone. Her marriage to Zaal had ended almost thirty years ago when he finally left her and now she was devoured by the pain of her choices.

Shattered.

I wish I had done it all differently, she thought as the tears began to fall. G and The helper looked on as her gurgled sobbing grew louder. The reel of her life, played in front of her and Nadia recalled all the moments she had made a choice she wasn't proud of:

Getting pressured into marrying Zaal

Ignoring every moment that told her he wasn't THE ONE

Not having kids because of him

Continuing to spend eleven hours a day at her job

Cutting off completely with her parents after her divorce

Stopping her night time ritual of talking to G, out of anger

And on and on

On that day, she let her tears fall freely. They gushed down uncontrolled, as the heart-ache she felt, made her realise – *It could have all been different.*

She could have chosen differently.

"I should have been braver... I wish I could go back. Please god. Please!"

Little did she know, her regrets were being acknowledged. Those magic words were being heard. Seeing Nadia realise the core of her mistakes, shifted something in her fate.

Her regret, and the clarity she had just gained, led G to do what he almost never did; he decided to give her a second chance, a RESET.

With a sudden flash of light, Nadia's world was filled with a blindingly weightless feeling. Everything stopped.

And before she realised it, Nadia was back in her mother's womb.

Her story reset.

And this was Nadia's second chance. This time round, she was becoming the braver version of herself – the one that developed the courage to listen to the difficult answers that lay within her. The one with the courage to trust.

"The second chance seems to be working," The helper said, grinning, relieved.

***

Over the next month, Zaal started sending Nadia nasty text messages, when she stopped answering his blisteringly angry calls. He even called up her parents in India, who then called her to try and convince her to take Zaal back and not 'end a good thing'.

In one message Zaal said: "I can't believe you are doing this to me after all I invested in you over the years. You're a real bitch."

Another said: "You will never be successful. You just don't have it in you and you know it. You need me or you will end up alone like your mother. I can take care of you. Don't be stupid."

Mom said: "Nadia stop flitting from one boy to the next like a butterfly. You are twenty six now. I was already married at your age."

Dad said nothing. No consolation, no chiding. He completely ignored that fact that Nadia had broken up with her boyfriend of three years. When she called him, they spoke of how he was planning on retiring, for one minute and twenty seven seconds. Then he handed the phone to Sabina Granny who wasn't keeping too well.

Sabina Granny said, "Oh you left that Zaal boy? Good call! He was so short. I think you need someone tall." She was trying to make Nadia laugh, and it had worked.

***

Waking up alone in the mornings did a funny thing to Nadia. For a couple of seconds every morning, she was free. And then suddenly she would recall all the hurt and loneliness that she had gone to sleep with. But for maybe one or two glorious seconds each morning, she got a glimpse into peace.

Before she remembered that she had just broken up with a man she loved. Before she realised she was in a job she dreaded going to. Before she realised she would not get touched by anyone that day. No loving snuggles. No one holding her hand. No text saying 'I love you sexy.' Before all this… she had a few seconds of peace.

And the funny thing is, she couldn't allow herself to become too aware of those seconds. The moment she became aware that she had those peaceful seconds, they would vanish. That was their nature. And then the day would begin.

She would reach the office, where she smiled and chatted and discussed everyone's weekend. Ohh the small talk; the bane of her existence!

They would discuss big data and e-commerce projections and why buyers return to buy a second pair of shoes and how soon they return for a repeat order etc. etc. etc. She would get to work by 9 am (in the winter, the sun has just about snuck out by then), and return home on a good day by 8 pm. There were entire weeks in the winter months when Nadia didn't see the sun except through the tinted windows in the office.

She had no energy left after work to do anything on most days, so meeting people was out of the question. Sundays was all she got to do her housework, grocery shopping, laundry and cook for the week. She hadn't even been to central park in eight months and she lived in Manhattan for crying out loud. She met her friends barely once in a month or so now, and even at those rushed catch up dinners, she was sleepy and thinking about the emails she had to reply to on the subway ride home. eWay had consumed her existence and the idea of a work-life balance, at this point, was LOL worthy.

But this was her job and she was good at it. It earned her good money and the people were sweet. It all added up, right?

Except for one tinsy winsy itsy bitsy miniscule thing – she had learned to trust her gut by now, and it told her a sad truth:

WTF is this nonsense. I don't care about selling shoes. I want to impact the world.

But how do you sign up for an 'impact the world' job? Are there any courses in Impactology at business school? And how much salary does the world give you for this impact, per annum? Does it come with dental benefits and flex hours?

At this job, she got a pat on the back every time she wowed her boss, and she could expense lunches with co-workers. Also, she was important to her company. Right?

At this job she earned good money and could pay for her expensive Manhattan studio. At this job she could dress up in formal wear and look chic. This job would make her 'successful' one day. And she knew this job. This was safe.

Do I just suffer from chronic dissatisfaction? Is that why I'm not satisfied with my job? Nobody can be and do and have everything, right?

"Yet another one haunted by this idea," God chuckled. They had seen this perceived limitation play out often, with many souls.

But would Nadia be any different?

***

A couple of days later, the end of season reports were due and it was a hectic day at work. Nadia was finishing up her report after working long and excruciatingly hard at making it perfect. After all, praise was her drug of choice. It gave her a high like nothing could.

No praise = no high. No high= that night she must face her life.

Facing her life= possibly crying.

To cry = she is not perfect.

She is not perfect = she can't love herself.

Ergo, Praise from others = Love for herself.

Fun question: Is it possible to love yourself if the people around you, don't praise you?

Rational answer: *I really don't have time to wonder about such asinine questions. I have a report to complete!*

And complete it she did. It was a thing of beauty. Everyone thought so. Her boss even ended his lengthy speech of praise with the line "Nadia, you really can do anything. Wow."

While she walked home from the subway that cold January night, the high of those words lifting her spirits, it rang in her mind.

I can do anything. I can do anything. I can do anything.

Almost like a chant; like one of those peppy, empowering songs by Taylor Swift or Beyoncé or Prince.

Tra la la la la la la I can do anything. Anything at all.

Wow la la la la la la I can do anything. Anything at all.

Dum da dum dee dum da dee,

I can be, I can be,

Anything!!

Her anthem, she had found. Self-coined and beautiful in its simplicity, this anthem stuck in her mind all night. She even heard it in her dream as she slept. She hummed it while taking a poop the next morning and all the way to work. Oh what a happy high it was.

As the anthem churned in her mind like the spin cycle in a washing machine that just won't stop, she thought about what it meant a little more. Was it possible? Could she maybe, perhaps, by any chance… leave her job?

Could she do something to impact the world?

Bahhhh. What a crazy notion. Who did she think she was? Gandhi? Nelson Mandela? Donald Trump?

What an ego I've developed! No. It is best to do what you know, and do it well.

"Jeez... Why does she think it is her ego talking to her. I never get any credit!" G pouted.

And so the self-doubt continued over the next month. The anthem stopped playing in her head, and her job went on.

Sure enough, the world kept rotating and revolving. The thing about the world is... it continues turning, even if we don't turn our world around.

"Do we let this continue...?" The helper asked when it got too painful to watch Nadia repeat the same shitty work day over and over again like a bad version of 'Groundhog Day'. Eternity had made him patient, but time was a-wasting and Nadia's calling was a-waiting... unanswered.

"Okay, hit her," God responded.

The helper obliged.

***

She had never felt pain like this before.

It was like a waterfall of agony rolling down her back. Lying down hurt, standing up hurt, coughing hurt, it seemed as if merely speaking, hurt. She called in sick to work that day, and the next and the next.

It was the last week of March, and everyone she knew was either out of town, or had family visiting them for Easter. Finally out of sheer desperation, she called her mother in India. Maybe she had some suggestion for a pain killer Nadia could try for her back pain or something. She had work pilling up at the office and her boss had already tactfully asked her to return 'soon'.

"Mom, I don't know what's wrong, but I'm scared. I'm in sooo much pain. I can't move. I need to go to a doctor and figure this out."

"You must be slouching at work. All those long hours at the laptop. I told you this would happen. Even my ankle has been bothering me again. This whole week I haven't slept."

"Oh no. Have you tried some medicine?" But she had heard it a dozen times before. Roxanne was in constant pain. Some ache here, some fall there and never enough sleep. Once she had heard Roxanne say to a new acquaintance "You know I have so much on my mind, I haven't slept in a year."

"All year?" he asked, incredulous. "Yes, it's horrible… but what to do. Such is life." And thus the Roxanne moto was reiterated – "What to do. Such is life."

On hanging up after an eight minute chat about Roxanne's ankle, because pity was what Roxanne hungered for, Nadia thought once again about who could help her. Dad? That would be an even more futile conversation than the one she had just had with Mom. Who could take her to a doctor? And more importantly why was her back killing her all of a sudden.

She wasn't willing to buy the 'such is life' logic she had heard all her childhood. If there is one thing she had learned from Roxanne, it was not to live like Roxanne.

Roxanne had stayed in a job she hated, in a marriage she hated, in a home she hated because 'such is life'. The job paid well and she might become boss one day and oh how prestigious that would be. And in the meantime, the sorrowful tail garnered lots of pity from everyone she encountered.

Roxanne believed she couldn't have more than that, and so she didn't.

And then it hit her like a bullet to the brain.

Unconsciously, Nadia had repeated that pattern. Eeks!!! She was doing what she said she would never do... live like her mother.

Ohhhh noooo!!!! I'm being like... Mom.

Goosebumps puckered her hands and spine.

And that did it.

No more.

Despite the pain, she got dressed, walked down, took a cab to the emergency room and got a check-up.

It was a slip disc. They gave her pain killers and a muscle relaxant and prescribed bed rest. On the cab ride home, Nadia composed her resignation email while humming her anthem. She was on a pain killer and sudden clarity 'high' this time.

Tra la la la la la la I can do anything. Anything at all.

Wow la la la la la la I can do anything. Anything at all.

Dum da dum dee dum da dee,

I can be, I can be,

Anything. Anything at all

I can have anything tra la la la la la la

Absolutely anything wow la la la la la la

I'm sure.

Yup! Definitely the pain killers talking. Right?

She lay in bed for the better part of three weeks after this, humming her anthem and inviting friends over to make the most of all the free time she now had. She also got back to writing her poems in her trusty journal.

"She has begun to practise going through her problems, not around them," The helper and G high-fived.

From baby steps, she had reached large leaps. Leaps of faith.

God Particle

By Nadia

Like the still water reflects the vast blue sky,
I want to reflect YOU.

But to see your shape, I must calm my mind,
Understand your heart and still mine.

Take some time off from my human race...
Maybe then I can mirror your exquisite face.

To reflect on your essence,
Would be a purpose so sublime,
I will spend lifetimes, if that's what it takes.
But the god particle in me, I must find!

***

In three weeks with physiotherapy and pain killers, Nadia's back healed and she was back to normal. Now it was time for the next step. When you land from a leap of faith, it can be disorienting. You need to take stock of your surroundings and often, you may end up with buyer's remorse. Getting the courage is sometimes the easy part. Keeping it; now that's a whole other deck of cards.

Luckily, after quitting her job, Nadia decided to take some time off to think. She needed time to reassess her options and make a thoughtful, well-informed career choice this time.

I don't want to rush into something just because... I can give myself some time. The risk is worth it, she told herself.

And then she saw him for the third time.

CHAPTER 11

SPRING

It was the first real day of spring in New York City. So far it had been a chilly April, but all of a sudden, that day it got warm. Nadia had heard rumours of the first cherry blossoms blooming by the mayor's house on East End Avenue and decided to walk up there and check them out.

She was sitting by the water and admiring the tiny light pink blooms, when she saw him in the distance. At first he seemed just like any other jogger, and there were many of them in that little park on that magnificent day. As he came closer, she noticed that he was totally out of breath. He was a couple of metres from her when all of a sudden, he almost fell over. He glanced her way while standing upright again, and as he huffed and puffed, she smiled at him.

It was a spontaneous smile. She didn't intend to smile at this stranger in the park, but he seemed familiar and quite frankly, comical, in the way he was trying so hard to appear composed, when he was obviously winded.

She knew he seemed vaguely familiar and the moment he smiled back at her, she recalled seeing him many years ago.

Ahhh…those dimples!

How uncanny! How could she remember his smile from eight years ago? It was the strangest thing. Smiling back, he sat down next to her, still panting.

"Give me a heads up if you're going to black-out, okay," she said with a mischievous grin.

He chuckled and continued breathing heavily.

After a good ten seconds he responded, "I'm running after a long time. I just didn't realise how out of shape I've gotten," he said a little embarrassed, "I used to do this route without needing to sit down."

"Well if it's any consolation, I needed the laugh. So thanks for losing your breath and balance in my presence," Nadia said, noticing how he subtly blushed when she looked him in the eyes this time.

And then he replied with words she would never forget, "You're welcome. I have a feeling your presence has a way of doing that."

Now it was her turn to blush. *WHOAAA. Is he being slick? Flirt-much?*

Yet, somewhere in the pit of her stomach, she felt it. It was telling her that he wasn't flirting. He wasn't saying what he thought she wanted to hear, like so many men do. He was simply stating a fact.

She looked away and scanned the trees again for a few seconds in an effort to distract herself from the awkwardness she felt. He did the same, but soon decided to talk again.

"You come here often?" he asked.

"Not really. I came here once before. Last year with my ex, and I remembered how stunning it is this time of year. Cherry blossoms make me happy."

"Yea me too. That's why I used to run here."

"So why did you take a break from running?" she asked, realising she genuinely wanted to know. This wasn't small talk. This felt like a catch-up of sorts.

"Well…" he paused and then spoke again with an odd look on his face; the kind of look you have when you are beginning to solve a tough math problem, but aren't sure if your method is correct yet. "What I tell people is I got busy and just don't have the time to run."

He paused, then continued slowly.

"But what I just realised is, it gave me too much time to think. Alone. And I was in a place in my life where I couldn't handle that."

"You needed space from you," she said with a knowing laugh.

"Yea I guess," he admitted, shyly.

"And how are you and you getting on now? Reconciled?"

"Beginning to, hopefully," he replied with an honest smile.

And she felt that feeling in her stomach again. She knew he meant it. This was no 'play' or charming line. He was being inexplicably and refreshingly, open.

She nodded and looked out at the water now. The sun was about to set and the ripples on the water were a soothing shade of pearl.

"So why did you need the laugh? I'm happy to fall again if it'll help," he joked.

"I may take you up on that," she said and continued after a few seconds, "Laughing isn't as easy anymore as it used to be. I think New York has done that to me."

It was a fact. Nadia wasn't bitter or upset about it, but it was a truth she had come to realise over the last few days. Over the last year, in the city of ambition, dreams and a million people, she had started to feel… alone. And things just weren't 'light' anymore. The lightness had left with Chris. The heaviness had slowly set in over the years and she didn't know how to shake it.

He didn't respond, but just kept looking at her. She continued "I quit my job recently and now…" She stopped, there was nothing more to say. The heaviness was visible.

"And now you need to laugh" he responded sensing her mood. "Hmmm let me see… knock knock…"

"Hahhaah. Who's there?"

"Booo"

"Booo who?"

"Don't be sad, it's just a joke!"

It took a second, but she unexpectedly, started laughing. Loudly, uninhibited, she laughed with him while the East River went from pearl to dusky, and the cherry blossoms got ready for their night's slumber.

Their meeting had been a lifetime in the making and this time they were both ready. Their hearts were open. G had made sure of it.

She felt lighter as the laughter died down, realising they hadn't asked each other's names yet.

"I'm Nadia by the way."

"I'm Arjun," he said shaking her hand & noticing her firm handshake.

"Desi, right?"

"Yea, couldn't you tell?"

"Actually, I could," she replied with a glint in her eye. "And I've seen you before, running, years ago."

"Really?? No way… I would have remembered meeting you."

"We didn't meet, we just passed each other on the street while I was at BCU."

"Ahh. That's possible because I went to…" His phone started ringing.

"Just a sec, I got to take this," he said, frowning now.

"Hi…Yea I'll be home soon. Met an old friend…"

He lied to whoever was calling him. *Why?* Nadia wondered, suddenly her antennas were up.

But one more thought caught her off guard. On hearing him say it – 'an old friend', it hadn't felt like a lie to her. Why?

"Sorry about that. I completely lost track of time. My…" (he paused for a quick millisecond, but she noticed it) "…girlfriend is waiting for me,"

It felt bizarre to hear that. His girlfriend.

"Oh no problem. I also got to get going," she said immediately, formal now. Her guard was up.

He didn't respond. He just sat there looking at her as if he couldn't move. As if he couldn't think or talk.

She stood up to leave but he still didn't move. He continued sitting there, watching her stand up.

Why is he being so odd, she thought. *Go home dude. Your girlfriend's waiting… should I say something or just leave?* she wondered, but couldn't figure out what to do next.

"Ummm…" she finally said, "Ok, bye," and she began to turn away when he blurted out – "Wait"

She turned around, a little annoyed now. But then she saw it – He looked wounded. Heavy.

"What's wrong?" she asked with concern in her eyes.

"I… I…" he stammered. Ten minutes ago he had been confident, witty and open. Now he couldn't get any words out. What was going on here?

"I'll be back for a run tomorrow," he finally said, "will I see you again? Maybe we can pick up where we left off?"

He said this almost pleadingly. As though he felt guilty, but desperate, all at the same time.

She sat back down not knowing how to respond. Why was he asking her to meet? They didn't even know each other AND he had a girlfriend. Was he just another F**k boy? And why did he look so worried. His tone had almost been a whimper at the end. And then she felt it once again. It nudged her.

She looked into his eyes and said, "Sure. See you tomorrow."

Then she smiled reassuringly at him, got up and walked away. The entire subway ride home she played this exchange over in her mind.

More than the words they had spoken, the way she had felt, stuck with her. She could rewind back to when he smiled at her and sat down. She had felt at ease immediately, as if a long awaited old friend had arrived. When Arjun spoke about not wanting to be alone, she had just understood. And when he asked her questions, she had opened up with no resistance. He just got it. How nice it had felt to be understood so easily.

But now she couldn't quite understand. Why had he wanted to meet her the next day? Why had she agreed? Was it just her loneliness...

But the idea of not seeing him the next day was.... unthinkable. She almost *needed* to. She had to make sure she hadn't imagined him up like a NYCM (New York City Mirage) for the 'connection starved'.

Did he really have the long slender limbs she had noticed today? Was his smile really that natural and unassuming? Could those dimples be real? Were his eyes really a hazel shade of honest?

She was restless all of the next day. There is only so much cooking while snacking on Reese's Piece's one can do as a distraction.

That evening, she returned to the bench by the East River and saw that he was already there, waiting. He smiled at her; a beaming smile, that once again disarmed her and took her restless jitters away. And oh those dimples.

"I'm so glad you came... so where were we?"

And they just picked up from last evening, as if no time had passed.

"Oh I think you were telling me about what school you went to..."

"Ahh yeah. I went to NYU but I visited my sister in Boston quite a lot. We are very close. She went to BCU too."

"Hhaahah small world. Did you guys ever eat at Nacho Mamas on Boylston? I'm suddenly craving their nachos."

"We ate there all the time! Now I'm craving them too. No place here makes nachos like that."

"I knowwww… they were like cheese covered chips of joy!!!" Nadia exclaimed.

And again they both laughed. For most people, nachos do not equal joy. For most people being silly with a stranger isn't normal. Clearly, this wasn't a 'most people' kind of encounter.

"You know what…" he said suddenly, "let's go." He stood and up and grabbed her hand, leading her away from the bench.

"Where are we going?" she asked, surprised, and a little excited. He had taken her hand. Her mind was racing and her stomach was churning with the happy tingles.

"For nachos," he said matter-of-factly.

As they walked to the road, she shyly wrenched her hand away and he instantly became aware of what he had done.

"Oh I'm sorry. I didn't mean to…." he stammered and turned a unique shade of ruby. Who knew brown people could turn *this* red?

"I shouldn't have just…"

"No no. Chill…come on, let's go," she said changing the subject. She acted like it was no big deal. Acted. But his touch had been a huge deal. They had held hands and walked for probably an entire minute, and it had felt… fitting.

The nachos were not even close to the ones at Nacho Mamas, but they didn't care. By the time they left the small Mexican place by Washington Square Park, it was 7:30 pm. It was a chilly day again; spring is so unpredictable that way. She shivered as they walked into Washington Square Park to cross it and turned to him. There was a piano playing somewhere.

"Do you want to sit a while? Listen to the music?" she asked him, taken in by the moment.

"Yea sure. Are you cold though?"

"A little," she smiled and said, "I didn't expect to be out this late or I would've carried my jacket."

He smiled back. "Take mine" he said, swiftly taking off his thin NYU sweatshirt and moving behind her to help her wear it.

"Thank you," Nadia said, feeling a warm sensation creeping in on her heart.

They sat down near the pianist and experienced the magic of that night for a few minutes. The cold breeze, the Washington Square monument lit up, the piano music and being near each other. He had sat down very close to her, maybe needing the body heat without his jacket. Or maybe there was another reason.

While at dinner, they had talked continuously, about their parents, friends, his job, her ex job, hobbies, their values, dreams etc. etc. but now they were quiet. Neither said a word. They only listened to the piano and the distant sound of an ambulance whining away.

"This is beautiful," She finally said, with happiness emanating from her.

He nodded and turned to her, not saying a word, but looking deep into her eyes. She held his gaze, mesmerised by the music and their connection.

Before she knew what was happening, they had both reached out and held each other's hand. In that instant, instinct had taken over. And they had let it.

They held hands and continued gazing into each other's eyes. They weren't giggly or joking around, the way they had at dinner. This was different. But in less than a minute it was over.

Nadia pulled away and broke his gaze.

She was the first to speak, "Soooo… it may be time to address the elephant in the park."

"Yup," he agreed, "I have a girlfriend," he admitted reading her mind.

"And you have spent the last three and a half hours with me… why?"

The moment called for directness. Why say in a million words, what you can say in one.

"Because... I felt like it," he responded looking down at his hands, almost like a school boy who had cut class. Clearly he subscribed to the no-nonsense philosophy of communication too.

"Why is that?"

Looking up, he smiled and turned the tables on her this time. "Why did you?"

TOUCHÉ

Slowly and with much consideration, she responded, "I'm not sure why. My gut told me to meet you again today. I did it because it felt... right."

She said it so frankly, as if it was completely normal to tell a guy you met for the second time, that spending time with him felt 'right'.

G was proud. This conversation would have taken many others, months to have. But not Arjun. Not Nadia. By now, they had both learnt not to avoid the truth, however strange, embarrassing or gooey it sounded.

But back to the elephant they had to discuss. Her name was Rebecca and she was lovely. Arjun told Nadia about Rebecca; how they had been together for a year. They worked together at EY and they practically lived together. He had loved her at first but over the last three months, he couldn't shake the feeling that something was off.

"And I don't know why I haven't told her all of this," he concluded, "or maybe I do."

She understood. Rebecca was his 'almost'. She never said that to him though. Some things you just got to figure out on your own. And then she knew what she had to do.

She stood up as he knew she would, and said, "Arjun, I don't want to complicate life right now. As much as I want to see you, I know it's the last thing you need right now. And I need to clear my head too. I guess this is it."

He stood up too, nodding, with that same heaviness she was familiar with, all over his face. They looked at each other for a second, almost as if they wanted to memorise each other's faces and then they hugged.

After that, they parted. She walked away. She walked away to help herself. She walked away to help him and do what was right. She didn't want to be the final straw in someone's break up, no matter how lonely she was. No matter how right it felt.

It was not who she was.

***

So she avoided East End Ave for the rest of the spring and focussed on her 'what next'.

The encounter with Arjun hadn't made her sad or disappointed though. In fact, it had shown her, once again, something crucial for the next phase of her life. That even after things ending with Zaal, and Chris passing away, and all the turns her life had taken in the last couple of years: She loved herself.

Not just liked herself or tolerated herself, (because she is the one person she can't escape) but truly loved herself. She loved how she had been brave with Zaal and Arjun. She loved how she had been brave and finally quit her job. She loved how she picked herself up after Chris.

She loved how she had faith in herself and knew she would find her calling. She loved that she even believed in having 'a calling' and falling in love and THE ONE, after the things she had experienced.

Growing up in a bitter, toxic home often kills one's faith in love, but not for Nadia. And she loved herself for all of this.

CHAPTER 12

SUMMER

With the summer came the rising heat. Just as in winter, when she crossed the street just to stay on the sunny side while walking, now she crossed the street often, to stay in the already crowded shade. Sweat oozed from her all day and in a weird way, she loved it. You can take the girl out of Mumbai, but you can't take the Mumbai out of the girl!

In Mumbai, Nadia use to live on a quiet-ish, tree lined street called Almeida Street, named for a Portuguese naval captain and explorer who helped secure the Bombay region for the Portuguese in the 1500s, when the now thriving city was just a group of seven islands that comprised of small fishing villages.

The street she grew up on was completely residential and a flute vendor visited it, every Sunday morning. One of Nadia's best childhood memories was waking up to the sound of the flute, on those warm mornings and lying in bed to the fading music as the vendor slowly walked on. She always wondered, *why does this guy visit every single Sunday? How many people buy flutes, after all?*

But maybe he just liked to play his melodies, while wandering those lazy streets at their most deserted hour.

For everyone was at home on a Sunday morning, in bed or eating breakfast, while he could walk by, providing his musical score. And now, Nadia understood this more. He got to do what he loved. That Sunday flute music was his contribution, however small it may seem to most people.

After waking up to the flute man, Nadia would sometimes head out with her cycle, to take advantage of the minimal traffic on Sundays. The wind on her face as she picked up speed, and the sway of the cycle as she balanced it, made her feel kind of in control and one with the wind. No Mom and Dad, no homework, no school mean girls, no biting remarks… just the wind and its human admirer – Nadia.

The wind made her feel free, alive, out of this world. And that was a feeling she treasured, even today. She would ride her bike to Haji Ali and park it by the waterfront, to gaze at the mosque in the water, while the wind worked its spell. And then she would get home and write.

Conversations with Wind
By Nadia

She blew by me and I felt her in my bones.
I grabbed her and said – "Hey, hold up... let's
chat a while. You intrigue me."
Her name was Wind (how very hippie chic).
Wind, who cannot be restrained.
Wind, who changes direction without warning
or forethought.
She looked irritated at my intrusion, and
replied,
"I can't wait here so you can get to know me...
got to keep on moving, lots to explore, lots to
know. I'm only me if I'm free."
"Don't you get lonely whooshing around? Let's
grab a coffee and a cuddle?"
"Hell no!" she said. Maybe loneliness was her
companion.
"You confuse me," I said to her; which she
understood perfectly well as she blew away.
But still intrigued, it led me to wonder:
What is she made of? Where does she come
from? Where will she go?
Who knows?
Probably not even Wind herself.
No one can grasp such invisibilities.
For the wind once seized... is nothing.

***

One day, early into the summer, as Nadia told Isla about her love of cycling as a child, the fitness enthusiast Isla suggested a swim at the local YMCA pool. She agreed and went with Isla, and then again without her. Once, twice, thrice and just like that, Nadia discovered a new love. How obvious it seemed, but it had taken Nadia twenty six years to discover that a person who loves water, will probably love swimming.

"Now water can teach her about letting go, " G said to The helper.

And so it did.

Slowly but steadily, she learned that if you are to stay afloat, gain speed and truly thrive in water, you have to make yourself one with it. The more you let go, the easier that gets.

Swimming gave her time to think, with all her senses calm. The water felt so good against her skin that it was almost a meditative experience.

Nadia would think about all the things she wanted to let go off – the loneliness she felt while growing up, the bitterness she felt towards her parents, the meanness she encountered in High School, the way she had pushed herself to cover up her emotions for most of her life, the sharp ache she felt whenever she remembered Chris, the regret she had at remaining quiet for years with Zaal, her fear of the future and what it would bring.

Almost like magic, while Nadia swam, all these coatings on her soul, started melting away. The chlorine water was leaching it all out of her muscles, bones, skin and soul. Leaching out all of the regret, shame, guilt, grief and rage, until all she felt was the cool water on her skin and the way the breath felt leaving her nostrils, and then entering again.

Nadia even made a list one night. Things I love about swimming:

1. I'm all alone (figuratively)
2. Nobody is looking
3. The water feels nice
4. Un-does my stress
5. The pool looks pretty
6. No distractions. Can't even listen to music
7. Makes me physically let go
8. Feels like a water-hug
9. Beats the heat
10. Regulates my breathing as if I'm meditating

Nadia swam, wrote poetry, cooked for friends and herself, and explored more and more of Manhattan almost daily. She used her free summer to shed a lot of the guck from the past. And as the guck left, the joy reappeared.

The joy began with the realisation that Nadia had something very, very rare – free time. Her savings could get her through another few months at least. The free time was also accompanied by the summer heat and the best city on earth to spend it in. She knew what she had to do!

She began to play 'discover' again. She would walk through the Conservatory Gardens in Central Park North, with its bazillion flowers in full bloom and dip her feet into the fountain, just sitting there for hours. She would spend the day by the Chelsea piers or read a book on a park bench in Morningside Park or even take the free Staten Island ferry up and down just for the impressive view. She even managed to sneakily follow a resident, and get entry into the 'forbidden for outsiders' Gramercy Park!

It was just like any other park, but made sweeter by her criminal-like entry. Joy was her companion on all these adventures. Joy and the watchful eye of G, of course.

"She is learning so many lessons," noticed The helper, "Moving fast."

"Getting ready for love will do that to you," God replied.

"I think it's because of her growing love for herself, no?" argued The helper.

To which G replied, "Chicken or egg?"

Two Way Street

By Nadia

I have no doubt you love me.
With the tremor of the pine leaves
I saw the sun filter through... and I just knew!

I know you are with me.
With every cool December breeze,
Every soft drop of rain,
I feel it... and I'm united with you!

Today, I looked on a seagull,
Flying overhead as if to survey me,
I saw it accompany me, and I knew... that's
You!

You find tiny ways, every day,
At the oddest hours, in the slightest ways,
To show me you are around.
And why would you, unless I did too.

I try to show you my love
With a kind word here and there,
A silent prayer in my heart,
A soft song whispered in the still air.

From day one, the murmur in my heart rang true.

And whenever there is ache, questions, uncertainties or doubt,

I'm reassured, there is also You.

CHAPTER 13

FALL

Nadia almost fell off her bed as the ringing awoke her at 3:17 am.

Who da f***....

But before she could complete the thought, the name flashed on her screen.

Sabina Granny

She usually never called. What had happened? Panicking slightly, Nadia answered:

"Hi Granny. What happened?"

"Nothing darling. What do you mean? And why do you sound so groggy?"

"Granny, it's 3 am here."

"Ohhh sorry! I never can quite understand this time difference. I'm always afraid I'll catch you at a bad time, like I just did."

"Hahah don't worry about it, Granny. What's up? I'm actually very happy to hear from you. Just today, I was thinking about home before I fell asleep."

"You still call Mumbai home? After all the years there."

"Y--Yea I guess. Didn't realise I was doing that," Nadia replied, a little embarrassed that her words had betrayed her inner feelings.

"Nadia, your dad told me you have quit your job. What are you doing there now?"

"Umm nothing as of now. Trying to find what's next actually. I want to take some time though and not just rush into anything."

"So why not do it here? At home."

She had never considered the option seriously. Nadia loved Mumbai, BUT with the city, came living with either one of her parents, and that was more than enough to drive mental peace far, far away. (In India it is almost blasphemous to live separately from your parents. Nobody ever moves out of their parents' home, until they are married. If they did, Indian society would spontaneously combust. Nadia couldn't be held responsible for that!)

So, moving back to Mumbai, wasn't an option for Nadia.

"Granny, ummm... my life is here now you know. Besides, the job market has more to offer here and..."

"I've heard these excuses from you for nine years now. But I know you, and I know the bottom line. You want to put an ocean between you and your parents. You think I don't know that?"

Stumped, Nadia replied, "You know how it gets at home. I can't live full time with Mom or Dad. It's just too much ya."

"That's exactly why I'm calling. Come live with me. Your Dad is moving to Goa for good. Retiring. And you can say that your poor old granny can't live all alone and needs you to take care of her. It's the perfect alibi."

At this, they both laughed, as only they could. Sabina understood Nadia in a very obvious manner for they had the same driving force in them. They both, at their core, wanted the same thing… to be free!

"Will you think about it, Nadia?" She asked when their laughter died down.

"Yes Granny. Thank you for calling. I miss you and… I'm mad at you for not calling me more often," She said in a mock complaining tone.

"Phone calls are not my thing, Nadia. You know that. You can't teach an old Granny new tricks. We will talk face to face when I see you next, okay?"

"Okay Granny."

"Now you sleep well, my baby."

"Mwaaah. Bye."

"Bye." And they hung up. Nadia stayed up all night contemplating the 'ifs' and 'buts' of her return HOME. Though, she didn't really have to decide whether or not she was going. Of course she was!

She knew that to put the puzzle of her heart together, she had to start at the start.

"The journey is beginning..." The helper said excitedly.

"Yes Nadia, keep going," G murmured.

CHAPTER 14

CLEANING OUT THE CLOSET

Nadia had been back a week when she began to realise how similar she was to her father. A couple of years ago, Akbar's mother, Sabina had moved in with him again. She was growing older and he was a very devoted son, though he didn't share her passion for collecting. His room in the house, which Nadia was staying in for the time being since he had moved to Goa, was sparsely furnished and neat. The rest of the house, however, courtesy of Sabina Granny, looked like a mild episode of *Hoarders*.

Granny hadn't thrown anything away for most of her life! There were cupboards all over the house filled with books, old newspapers, crockery, curios, artefacts and pretty much every piece of clothing any family member had ever owned. It was a large apartment by Mumbai standards, but cluttered beyond belief.

How can Granny live like this? No wonder dad finally moved away.

But Granny seemed to add more junk to the growing collection every day. She sat up most nights, cutting up the newspapers from that day, and filing the articles into appropriate files and folders. She had a file for important events in Mumbai, another for crimes against women, another for scientific progress, another for ocean and marine life related news (they had this passion in common), another for any news on climate change and so on and so on. It was her belief that she would one day need to refer to something she had read and therefore needed them all close at hand, in files, lost in the maze of 'old junk' that had become her house.

There was a lot of humour in it actually, and Nadia saw it. She had come to the house of the forgotten newspaper cuttings and all things throw away worthy, to gain clarity.

Maybe Granny has a file on it somewhere.

Since Nadia was free most of the day and most of her old friends, Payal included, had moved away, abandoning Mumbai like the uber expensive, sinking ship it seemed to be becoming (courtesy climate change), Nadia had a lot of time on her hands. She read, ate tons of yummy home-cooked food, wrote poems as usual, and she and Granny chatted a lot.

Nadia had never had this opportunity growing up, as time with Granny was always also time with her father. They never spent any time just the two of them, so now she discovered that Sabina sans Dad, was quite a naughty lady. She was like a teenager most days. They ate junk food, binge watched TV shows and gossiped together. And then Sabina had her adult days, where she went for funerals of friends and far off relatives being taken away by the pitiless joke that is ageing.

"I have nobody left from my old life you know," Sabina said one day.

"Nobody who knew me when I was young and free. It's almost as if those years didn't happen at all. I can't reminisce about them with anyone. I've attended so many of my friends' funerals… it feels extremely bizarre for me because I feel young, but I know that everyone around me is old and dying."

"What about Dad?" Nadia asked, feeling sad that Granny was sad. "He knew you when you were younger. You were young when he was born right?"

Granny exhaled slowly. "Yes I was twenty two when he was born. Too young. I didn't know what it meant to be a mother, to be responsible for another life like that."

"But I bet you were a great mom. You are so cool and understanding with me."

Sabina paused for a second or two and then slowly said, "Yes, *now* I am understanding and cool. But you were born when I was in my late forties. Unfortunately your Dad had a different version of me while he was growing up. And his father passing away when he was so very young, put even more pressure on me. I look back and sometimes wish I had done things differently."

"I've never heard you talk like this before granny. I knew dad lost his father early on, but… but I'm sure you did the best you could."

"Oh yes, that's true. I did the best I could at that time. And we all do I suppose. But…"

"But what?"

And then Sabina began to tell her everything. She told Nadia how Akbar had been an unwanted child growing up and how Sabina had resented him for keeping her in that life – the life of a single mother. She was too young and didn't know how to be a mother. She couldn't give him the love and attention a child deserves.

She told Nadia how he was raised by maids and nannies, and how the regret of all those years has been eating her up.

"But I know I was doing the best I could have. We all are Nadia. Remember that. So is Roxanne and so is Akbar. They just don't know any better, like I didn't. I couldn't give Akbar, what I didn't have. And therefore he hasn't been able to give it to you."

"Give me what Granny?" she quietly asked, though she knew full-well.

"My baby, Akbar couldn't be a good father to you because he doesn't know what that means. He doesn't know that a parent has to fight for their child. I didn't do that for him and he didn't do that for you."

Sabina paused as Nadia looked at the floor, not wanting to make eye contact while the emotions in her were rising up.

"I feel guilty about it and I KNOW he does too."

On hearing this, Nadia looked up. Her eyes met Granny's and then she couldn't hold it in. Tears started gushing down her cheeks as she finally said what had been caught in her heart for many years

"I always feel that Dad wants a life without me. As if he would wish me away, if he could… as if, if not for me, he could have a clean slate. That's why he meets or talks to me as little as possible! Just enough, but never more. Why won't he let me IN…?"

Sabina jumped in to answer, as Nadia started to ugly-sob and yelled out the last word.

"Nadia, he isn't 'in' himself. He *can't* let you into his heart. It's too tightly closed by guilt and shame and fear. His childhood, marriage and all the building bitterness has done that to him. But he loves you. I know that."

But Nadia's tears continued. The answer made sense, but…

Eventually her crying subsided and Nadia left Sabina to go to bed early that night. Tired from all the weeping and with the new information Sabina had given her, she fell right to sleep.

In her dream that night, she played with a furry black puppy on the beach. They ran around and wrestled and swam. It was a very fun day and she awoke feeling refreshed. The heaviness of last night was only a memory now. In the morning light, still lying in her bed, Nadia knew she was loved. Loved by a man who had many battles he was fighting and maybe losing, but she was loved. That knowledge would have to be enough for now.

Baby steps, she thought to herself with a small smile.

Rising out of bed, Nadia decided to clean it all out that day. It was time to declutter her soul, and what better way to do it than start with her surroundings. Sabina was in for a rude shock when she discovered her grand-daughter sitting on the floor in the passageway of the apartment at 8:23 am, going through the dusty contents from one of fourteen cupboards that lined the passage.

"Granny, I need to do this," Nadia said, as soon as she saw Sabina, knowing she would not be pleased.

"All of this has got to go! No more unnecessary clutter in this family."

And with that, she turned back to the file in her hand, leaving Sabina gaping, anxious, and quite annoyed. But she let Nadia do it, nonetheless. The conversation from last night had turned something in Sabina as well.

It took Nadia four and a half days of sitting with a bandana tied over her nose and mouth, to get through all fourteen dust-filled cupboards. The dust had given her a hoarse cough, but she persevered because at the end of every day, she felt just a little lighter. As if the stack of papers thrown away every day, were lightening her heart, a milligram more at a time.

Apparently, empty cupboards = happier Nadia

Dad would be pleased.

***

On day five, just as she was finishing up with the last cupboard in the row, she came across some of her Mom's things in a box. Clearly, this cupboard hadn't been opened since before Nadia was sixteen, because that is when Roxanne and she had moved out of this apartment. Maybe Mom had forgotten some stuff here, all those years ago.

She opened up the box labelled 'Roxanne Billimoria' (her mother's maiden name) and found something she hadn't known existed – Her mother's childhood journals, volumes one through six!!!

Mom used to journal? That doesn't seem like a Roxanne type of thing to do at all.

The handwriting inside made Nadia laugh. It was scratchy and childlike; completely different from Mom's handwriting today. The journals started when she was roughly twelve years old, and ended a year or so later.

She had one year of Roxanne's life in her hands! This would make for an interesting read. *What was mom like back then? Was she silly and annoying like the stereotype of a teenager? Did she have a childhood crush? Did she have bad spellings?*

A kazillion questions swarmed through Nadia's mind. She closed the last cupboard, went straight to her bedroom, where she plonked her behind into her bed.

Being cosy is vital to reading anything entertaining, and your mom's childhood diaries, definitely qualify. Her heart was beating fast because it felt just a little wrong. Voyeuristic.

But she hadn't been this excited about something 'bad', since her first snatched kiss in the elevator at school with Jay when she was seventeen. Those three seconds had been chock-full of quick fluttering butterflies and a fast heartbeat, just like now. And so she started reading…

Thursday 1st June, 1972

Darling Diary,

Yesterday was my birthday. I am now 12 years old. You are a present from Mummy. She says I should write in you often so I can improve my writing talent. And next year mummy wants me to read a famous diary written by a girl my age called Anne. She says it will make me smarter.

As a present Daddy took me to Juhu beach this evening and we ate ice-gola. Juhu is very far away and we had to take the train and a rickshaw which was bumpy. Mummy couldn't come as she had work to do. I told Daddy that we could go on Sunday so that even Mummy could come with us, but he said she wouldn't come even on Sunday, so we better finish it off. He had promised me months back that my birthday treat would be at Juhu Beach.

The beach was khali-khali when we reached. Some beggar children were playing in the water and I felt like joining them. It looked like so much fun but my dress would have got all wet.

In one corner of the beach I saw a pretty woman sitting with a box on her lap. I went over to get a better look and it had these colourful cards in it and we started talking. She was very sweet and let me hold the cards and see the pretty pictures on them. Some were scary like a man with swords in his back, but there was this one card that I loved the most. It had a woman on it and she was smiling & petting a lion! She had a sleeping number 8 above her head and at the bottom of the card it said 'Strength'.

Daddy came over to us to see what we were doing and the lady asked if she could read my cards. I didn't understand because I don't have any cards so how could she read my cards?

Daddy said no, even though I was curious to know what she meant. Before we could talk more, Daddy said we should walk on the beach and off we went, leaving the lady with the box behind.

We walked on the beach and I even dipped my feet in the white frothy part of the waves. Then we came back home. Mummy was in her room working and Dina & Farah were already asleep so I went straight to bed. Daddy went into his bedroom and slept too.

What a fun birthday treat I've had!

Love,

Roxy

Sunday, 4th June

Darling Diary,

Today all six of us ate lunch together. Mummy was reading the newspaper in the sun to get vitamin D. Cyrus was playing chess with Dina and he beat her at it again. I don't know why they even play because Dina gets very upset when she loses. Farah and I helped set up the table and serve the food that the cook made.

Daddy has taught the cook to make a mutton stew just like his mummy used to make. Farah and Dina say that their mother too is a very good cook. I've only met her once when she came to drop them off at our house last year. Mummy had placed an advertisement in the newspaper to help poor Parsis who couldn't take care of their children. Mummy says that there are a lot of poor Parsis even in Bombay who can't feed their children and it is our duty to help them. I just wish we didn't have to have Dina and Farah live with us, because now it's four of us children and I liked it better when it was only me and Cyrus. I have to share my bedroom & all my things with them and they sometimes dirty my clothes while playing. Dina tore my green skirt last week and didn't even say sorry even though Daddy told her to. Dina even lied to daddy and said that I made-up the whole thing and tore the skirt myself to get her into trouble. Why would I tear my own skirt?

She and Farah haven't spoken to me for a week now because I complained to Daddy about the skirt. I feel sad when they don't talk to me and I even promised them I would never ever complain to mummy or daddy if they started talking to me again.

Sometimes I wish I had a real sister so I wouldn't feel left out. Dina and Farah have each other. Cyrus has Mummy. Daddy has his friends. But I have nobody who likes me best.

At least now I can talk to you Diary.

Love,

Roxy

Wednesday, 7th June

Darling Diary,

I hate being the youngest!! I just hate it! Everyone treats me like a bai, always telling me to fetch things or do things for them. And everyone leaves me out of everything. Dina, Farah and Cyrus all got to go for a play with Mummy this evening at the Royal Opera House and I am left at home with the cook. How mean!!

Mummy said the play would go above my head. Then why can't I carry a small cushion and sit on it like I do when we go to the Talkies, to make myself taller in my seat.

They just purposely went without me. Even daddy went to his friend's house today and left me all alone. I hate when they do this.

And I know they are going to discuss the play all week now and stupid Farah will purposely talk about it in front of me to make me jealous. I don't like her. She always makes me feel dumb. As if I don't know anything.

They have only been here a year and already I can tell that Mummy likes them more than me, even though I do everything Mummy wants. I am studying so hard all the time and reading all the books she tells me to and I even sit and listen to the news on the radio with her. Why does she like them better then?

Why do I have to be at the bottom? In all my friend's families, they are the favourite in the house. All except me. I hate it.

Love,

Roxy

***

Two missed meals and an all-nighter later, Nadia had read them all. Devoured them, like an emaciated bear who had just awoken after a lonnnggggg hibernation.

Two things were very apparent after this first reading:

1. Roxanne had been utterly neglected as a child. Often treated with cold disregard.

2. She had developed a belief that she was somehow always 'less'.

Over the years, Nadia had shed a lot of tears because of Roxanne, but this was the first all-nighter she spent crying *for* Roxanne. For the first time ever, while Nadia read her mother's innocently painful journal entries, her mother had been freed from the burdensome title of 'mother', with all its expectations, pressures and ache filled memories.

That night, Nadia saw Roxanne, just as a person. In fact, not even a person, but a child. Nothing more. And that allowed the compassion to pour right out of her eyes.

As one neglected little girl understands another, Nadia felt Roxanne's angst through those pages. And with each diary entry, she understood the formation of the person, she now knew.

Things were falling into place like they never had before, and just like with her dad, Nadia figured out a very basic and crucial truth – *What Mom didn't get, she couldn't give to me.*

Almost instantaneously she stopped judging and resenting her mother. Instead, she was just filled with this quiet gratitude, that despite her own childhood experiences, she believed, wholeheartedly, in herself, and in the power of love. It always had and always would live deep inside her, no matter what life brings.

"That is her biggest strength," G said.

The helper knew this too.

They had watched Nadia forever, and at her lowest points, she had always cried out for help – for love. So they sent it.

Through all the baby steps, her faith in love, had caused the most gigantic leaps. Just like the one that night.

The Girl Inside
By Nadia

Beneath all the useless pride,
And the peels of various personalities,
You are just a little girl.
A little girl like me.

Beneath all the judgement & criticism,
All the obligations and scar tissue ,
You are just a little girl.
A little girl who doesn't feel seen.
A little girl like me.

Under the skin of self-protection,
And years of building up this facade
Despite all you say & all you do,
You are just a little girl;
Needing attention and some TLC.
A little girl like me.

Inside, where the void lives,
Where it breeds and grows,
Where all the pain lies dormant,
Waiting to rear its head at the slightest
provocation.
You are just a little girl,
It is clear to see.

Causing hurt, won't help you heal.
Anger and resentment are purposeless fiends.
Now shed that skin; it's too lived in.
And together let's be
Two little girls dancing carefree.
The way every little girl wants to be.

***

At 8:30 am the next day, almost nineteen hours after she had begun the journal voyeur session, Nadia fell asleep. For the next three days, she didn't do much else.

Sleep ---- Re-read ---- eat a little ---- sleep ---- repeat

Finally, when she had read all six volumes a solid three times, she put them back in the box and locked them away in her cupboard. They had been read, digested and assimilated. Now it was time to act.

She went over to mom's house for dinner that night. And for the first time in her entire life, she found the things mom said and did... funny. They didn't bug her or make her sad. It was just funny. Not a 'ha-ha' funny, but a more like 'that's mom' type of funny, where she simply accepted the way her mother was.

She was a person to Nadia now. She was allowed to be flawed and make mistakes; no longer held up to the pristine, high standards of being a 'Mother'.

They actually chatted and shared laughs that night. And after dinner, Nadia said what she had come to say, what she needed to say; what Roxanne needed to hear.

"Mom I have something I want to tell you. It's important and I want you to let me say it all. Please don't interrupt me because I don't want to miss saying anything."

"Ookkayyy… what's wrong?" Roxanne asked, as she crossed her hands across her chest, already becoming defensive.

Turning her chair to Roxanne and moving a little closer, Nadia began, "I want you to know that I love you. Unconditionally. Our relationship is very important to me and I will work on it more from now on. I will be honest with you about things I don't like and fight with you if I must. I owe us that. I know that you have had a hard life with your parents being the way they were, Dad and you not working out, and raising me pretty much single-handedly. And I appreciate it all and I am here for you. There is nothing that can make me stop loving you."

Roxanne just sat there, stunned, mesmerised almost. She didn't even blink!

"Mom, did you hear me?" Nadia asked after a couple of seconds, for Roxanne never didn't say anything. Silence was not her thing.

She nodded, still quiet. After a good five seconds or so, she said, "I love you too but I don't know what you mean. Why are you saying this to me? Are you trying to say there is something wrong with our relationship?"

Nadia just smiled, and calmly responded, "No Mom. It's just something I wanted to say. Now I'm going to head back home. Let's meet again in a day or two?"

"Sure. Okay," Roxanne replied, visibly confused.

Nadia smiled the whole drive home. She had expected her Mom to have a defensive response to her little soliloquy. And it was okay, for Nadia had learned to understand Roxanne.

It had been said and that is what matters.

Somewhere, somehow, it would trickle in, she knew. Baby steps.

CHAPTER 15

OPENING THE DOOR

Nadia had been lazing around all day, trying to decide whether or not she wanted to go to Goa to meet her dad. She had been back home for almost a month now and hadn't seen him yet.

After all her efforts to procrastinate were exhausted, she finally went online that day and booked her flight to Goa. She had two days before she would be face to face with Dad. She knew there were several difficult, but important conversations in front of her, and the daily beach visit she had promised herself, and all the drool worthy Goan food were the silver linings to this looming cloud of honest communication.

As it often did, her mind went back to Mom's journal and the things she had read there. Since she had read them, little-little things kept creeping back into her mind for her to mull on. It was like she was a cow, chewing the cud of all of this new information.

This time the thought that popped into her mind was of Roxanne's first entry in her journal. She got curious about that encounter twelve year old Roxanne had had with the lady on the beach.

What were those cards on the beach that day?

A man with swords in his back? Huh?

A lady petting a lion?

Was all of this just a child's over active imagination?

So Nadia did what most people do nowadays when they are in doubt. She Googled it. She typed 'card with a man with swords in his back'.

She expected nothing definitive to show up. Probably just random pictures of playing cards or swords or men with swords (King Arthur style), but she was not expecting what she saw.

The page was filled with the words 'Tarot' and 'Ten of swords' and 'occult'. And then she saw the image.....

(Google the image....Ten of swords.....seriously!)

Whoaaaa Whooaaa Whoaaa. The dude had ten swords in his back!!!!

Nadia. Couldn't. Stop. Staring.

After the initial shock wore off, she began to take in all the details of the card. There was a man on the ground, with ten swords, neatly piercing his back. No blood left the wounds though. You couldn't see his face and he lay on a shore somewhere with water, and then mountains in the background. The sky grew from yellow to black. Ominous, but yet with a sliver of hope; She didn't know why she felt that way when she looked at the card. There is no way that a dude with ten swords sheesh-kebabing him could have any hope, Right?

The card had ten written at the top in roman numerals and SWORDS on the bottom.

Way to be obvious Tarot. And then a funny thought hit her.

The dude kinda looked like a man asleep on a massage table with that red cloth neatly draped over his lower body. The ten swords looked like acupuncture needles because only their tips, seemed to be inside him. And there was no blood leaving the wounds. Maybe this wasn't such a grim situation after all. Who wouldn't want a massage and acupuncture, by a lake!

She had done acupuncture in New York three times to rid her of a shoulder pain that had taken a hold of her a couple of years ago, right after Chris left. It had worked like a charm, despite how alarming it appeared.

She was intrigued and decided to delve a little deeper. She had vaguely heard of Tarot in a 'one of those hocus pocus things' kind of way. But she had never seen a card or known anybody who used tarot, up till now.

Wikipedia led her further down the rabbit hole. She read:

"The **tarot** (/ˈtærou/; first known as **trionfi** and later as **tarocchi**, **tarock**, and others) is a pack of playing cards, used from the mid-15th century in various parts of Europe to play games such as Italian tarocchini and French tarot. In the late 18th century, it began to be used for divination in the form of tarotology/cartomancy."

So naturally she then searched for the word 'Divination' and read:

"**Divination** (from Latin *divinare* «to foresee, to be inspired by a god»,[2] related to *divinus*, divine) is the attempt to gain insight into a question or situation by way of an occultic, standardized process or ritual."

Immediately it jumped out at her- 'To be inspired by god.'

How do these cards inspire you? How are they at all connected to the big G?

And isn't the word 'occult', the opposite of God or divine. Isn't it like related to magic or scary movies and stuff? Confusing much!

The Wiki search for the word 'occult' yielded:

"The **occult** (from the Latin word *occultus* "clandestine, hidden, secret") is "knowledge of the hidden."[1] In common English usage, *occult* refers to "knowledge of the paranormal," as opposed to "knowledge of the measurable,"[2] usually referred to as science. The term is sometimes taken to mean knowledge that "is meant only for certain people" or that "must be kept hidden", but for most practicing occultists it is simply the study of a deeper spiritual reality that extends beyond pure reason and the physical sciences."

Hmmmmm…. Well, in a sense, God and spiritual things do fit the description of 'extending beyond pure reason and the physical sciences.'

This was, surprisingly, making sense to her.

Nadia had never given all of this that much thought. For her, her faith came from her heart, not her head.

It could be summed up in the simple feeling of love and joy she felt when she thought about G. To her, God just meant her all-knowing, all-seeing and all-understanding Best Friend. Nothing more. She believed that G wasn't scary or intimidating or judgemental.

And yeah, I guess that does go 'beyond pure reason'.

Once again, Wikipedia had given her some much-needed information.

That night, Nadia spoke to Sabina about her new curiosity with Tarot.

"Ah yes. I always found the cards very pretty. Purely from an artistic perspective. The images are very elaborate and attractive. I remember one of my classmates in art school had done her final thesis project on interpretations of Tarot cards. "

"What a cool idea. Have you ever known anyone who has done tarot though? Like gotten a 'reading' I think they call it."

"I don't think so, Nadia. You know me. Even if someone I know has done it, they would never tell me. Everyone knows my feelings on matters like this."

Sabina had always been averse to anything on the fringes of tangible. She was only concerned with what she could see, touch and taste. Everything else was nonsense. Just entertainment for bored, gullible or less than intelligent people. And she was definitely not one of them. No Sir-ey !

These opinions of hers did not fly with her religious relatives, who had slowly distanced themselves from her. Her sarcastic disapproval had been apparent and eventually, they grew tired of it.

But this was Nadia she was talking to. She didn't speak to Nadia that way. She had come to respect Nadia's sensitivity, even admire it.

"I'm very curious, Granny. It may be fun to give it a shot," She said with a coy smile, goading Sabina.

"So give it a shot then," she replied, not taking the bait, but ending the conversation by saying,

"Maybe your Dad will know someone. Ask him when you go to Goa. You know how hippy-dippy Goa has become."

CHAPTER 16

THE RUSH

Three days of laying out in the sun and bobbing up and down in the ocean later, Nadia had a colour to match the brown sands of Goa. She wondered why she hadn't come here sooner. It had actually been quite pleasant visiting Dad this time around. He had a full life and seemed very at-ease in Goa. She could hang out on a beach, reading all day, and then catch up with him and friends of his, at night for dinner. It was easy. Somehow Dad was a happier person now, and it showed.

Something about him is more... honest.

One night, Nadia was out for dinner with her father and an Israeli expat couple who he had befriended. The conversation turned to yoga and meditation and before she knew it, Nadia had asked them if they knew anyone who did Tarot.

They did. They found it surprisingly accurate.

Would you like to go?

Yes.

Here is the Tarot reader's number.

And the appointment was made. She lived in a town house near Carmona Beach in the south. It would be quite the drive, but Nadia was excited.

"Last time she ignored all the signs we gave her," said G, recalling how all the hints they had given Nadia even while she was on her honeymoon with Zaal and for the first few years of her marriage had been consistently overlooked. Since Nadia didn' t heed them, eventually her gut went quiet. She never came to live with Sabina Granny and never found her mother' s journals. She never tried to reconnect with her father. And never found her true calling.

"But this time it' s different. Her heart is focussed on changing. She is noticing..." The helper was happy his efforts weren' t going in vain in this Reset.

***

The Tarot reader Susan's house was in a typical Goan expat colony, where most of the homes remained unoccupied for several months of the year, but filled up in the winter when foreigners fled the cold of their lands, and moved to cheap and warm Goa. The grass was dry as the sun beat down on the small lawns in front of every townhouse, little kids played by the common pool and a steady breeze reminded you that you were the customary 500 metres away from the ocean.

She rang the doorbell of townhouse no. 45 and was greeted by the cleaning lady who led Nadia into a home office room with a giant bookshelf that covered one entire wall. A quick glance revealed titles she had never heard of- '*The Emerald Tablet*', '*Alchemy- The Art of Getting All You Desire*', '*Shiva's Mountain Home*' and so on. The theme was pretty apparent; Susan clearly loved reading metaphysical and esoteric literature.

In the centre of the room was a desk with a chair on either side of it. There was a beautiful lilac scarf set out on the desk with a pack of tarot cards lying face down on it.

The French doors looked out at the small backyard that had a herb garden and a lazing Doberman. In the corner by the door, was a large jar candle. It smelled of roses and filled Nadia's senses as soon as she entered the room. The walls of the room were utterly bare except for a clock.

While Nadia was admiring the Doberman through the window, Susan entered.

"Hi, I'm Susan."

"Hey, I'm Nadia. Thanks for seeing me at such short notice. I've never done anything like this before."

Susan's smile grew. "Well, then let's dive right in. I'm sensing energies of change coming off of you. Also, I sense a loving presence around you. You are being guided by a soul you knew in this life. Seems young and male. Any idea who it could be?"

"Huh…." Talk about being thrown into the deep end. Nadia didn't know what had hit her.

Energies?

Loving presence?

Soul she knew?

How could this lady have possibly known about Chris? And Susan hadn't even touched the cards yet.

"Umm…well my friend from university passed away a couple of years back. We were very close."

"And what does he have to do with water?" Susan enquired.

Slowly Nadia replied, flabbergasted "He was an oceanographer."

"I see. Well he is around and is looking out for you. You have an old connection with him and his energy is staying around you, to make sure you use the lesson you learned with him."

"I don't know what you mean." Nadia responded, choking back the tears that talking about Chris had brought forth. This was a little too much!

"Don't worry about it. I suggest you take notes now and later, you can think about what I said today. It will all make sense at the right time," Susan said with a surety in her voice.

"Okay. I'll try that," Nadia replied as she started to voice record the session on her phone like a good student. Gradually, her tears stayed in her eyes and the emotions subsided a little.

"I'm going to start the Tarot now. I want you to close your eyes and say a prayer. Any prayer. I will do the same and then we will begin."

"Okay."

Susan held the cards between her palms and closed her eyes. Nadia didn't though. She watched her mumble a prayer while holding the cards. Then Susan started to shuffle the cards, all the while, concentrating deeply with her eyes closed.

She opened her eyes and without even looking at Nadia, started laying them, face up, on the lilac scarf, in a pattern resembling a train, just one after the other.

It was almost a hypnotising experience. Nadia was enchanted by the cards, their colours, beauty and mystery. It is one thing to see something on a laptop screen, but to actually see the tarot cards in front of her and feel their energy, was an experience she would never forget.

Whaaat the... this does not feel normal.

Nadia kept watching Susan lay down one card after the next. And then she chuckled aloud as her mind gave her the answer – *Its para-normal, silly.*

"Did you say something?" Susan asked, looking up at Nadia's chuckle.

"No No. Sorry to interrupt you. I just had a funny thought."

Smiling, Susan began:

"This is a year of transition for you. Ending one karmic cycle and beginning another. The cards tell me that you are mourning this change, but there isn't any need to. Take it as a metamorphosis. It is essential and will bring you stability and happiness. Use this time for learning, rejuvenating yourself and spending time with family. See this card, Strength." And Susan held up the lion and lady card that Nadia instantly recognised from the description she had read in her mother's childhood journal.

(Google the image…Strength Tarot Card)

What struck Nadia, when she looked at the card up close, was the wreath of roses the lady wore on her head. She looked like a rose queen!

"It is sending you a message – love can do anything."

Nadia liked the sound of that. She didn't know what exactly Susan was referring to, but she understood the essence of the card and its message. The lady was petting the lion which would have been scary or even deadly for most people, but the lady on the card was doing it. Not with any physical strength or defiance, but rather with a gentle, loving look in her eyes. She almost seemed to tame the lion with her gentleness.

Nadia would remember this card often in the years to come and call on its message to guide her actions – the strength of Love.

Susan went on, "Also, this is a time for truth. Lots of new information coming your way and it is going to require courage and love on your part, to deal with it all."

"You can ask me specific questions now."

"Ummm. Sooo I quit my job a few months back. I know that wasn't the career for me but I don't know what is."

"That insight is coming to you very soon. I would say, it will be clear to you in the next week. Also, I don't see you as doing any one thing. You aren't the traditional 9-5 career type. You are extremely intuitive, so hone that skill and use it. Meditate on the question. You are definitely meant to be in a creative field."

A creative field? I'm not at all artsy, Nadia thought while Susan laid out some more cards on the already busy pile before her.

"I also see love entering your life very soon."

Ooooo!! Now this is juicy. "Really? I haven't even been dating," Nadia responded.

"You have met him already. It is an old, old bond. Lifetimes probably."

"I have no clue who you are talking about," Nadia said honestly, because Arjun had slipped into the 'never going to happen' recesses of her mind, being disqualified from her heart, for having a girlfriend. Also, she was in Goa now and he was in New York, so...

"Good thing we figured out how to make the world an even smaller place now with this social media thingy," G said to The helper.

"Give it some time." Susan replied. "He is definitely on the cards."

"Ohhhh is that where that phrase comes from? On the cards," Nadia suddenly asked.

To which Susan responded with a laugh, "Could be. I never thought of it actually."

"Ya me neither. It just struck me when you said it. I love finding out where old phrases come from. Or learning any cool new thing basically."

"Then you should learn tarot," Susan said taking Nadia by surprise. "There is a ton of information in these cards that can help you a lot. Even just as a hobby."

Nadia smiled awkwardly, paused and then slowly replied, "I…I don't know. I don't know anything about this world and I'm not even sure I fully believe in Tarot, to be honest. I don't know how this works."

"Oh that's easy – Energy. Intuition."

Nadia still looked bewildered, so Susan went on.

"While reading your cards, intuition flows through me. Tarot is one of the languages of the messages the universe wants to send you. So, the message I see on the cards, I translate into English for you."

"Sooooo someone is in your head telling you what to say to me?" Nadia questioned, perplexed.

"No no. I'm not possessed!" Susan chuckled. "The universe sends its messages for you, in the cards. I just read them out for you. That's all."

But Nadia was still confused and a little uneasy with the conversation by then.

Susan gave it one last ditch effort.

"The universe is an information database, Nadia. Like the internet. Tarot is like the computer and I am the screen. I make the info accessible to you."

Finally, it clicked. Nadia understood this millennial-suited explanation perfectly!

"Ohhhh I get it! I'm still not sure if I want to learn. But I get it."

"That's okay. Do you have any other questions for me?"

"No... I think that is all. This has been fun."

"One last thing. I see a Rose on the cards – a person you have to learn a skill from right away. Who is this person?"

"Rose? Hmmmmm... I can't figure that out. I don't know any Rose, if it's even a name....I'll think on it though."

"Okay then, I think we are done," Susan said moving her chair back.

"Thanks so much Susan," Nadia said. "You have given me lots of food for thought."

"My pleasure!"

After paying Susan for the session, Nadia was off. The entire car ride home she played the dual role- the sceptic v/s the curious.

At home she made a list titled: 'Food for thought' and wrote down all the things Susan had said, that hadn't quite made sense to Nadia – transition year, metamorphosis, her lover to be, their 'lifetimes' connection, her creative career to come and finally, the rose.

The tarot session had given her more questions than answers! Mulling this over, Nadia went onto Instagram for a browsing session. Nothing like mindless social media to distract you from thinking.

One notification.

As soon as she saw it, she had butterflies. No wait, much more than butterflies; she had dragonflies, or even real dragons fluttering around in her belly when she saw one follow request waiting for her. From: @arjunmodi

CHAPTER 17

ARJUN MODI

As excited, thrilled and curious as Nadia was on seeing a picture of Arjun, she was also just a little concerned.

What if he is still 'Arjun (I have a girlfriend) Modi'? What if this is just about sliding into my DMs.

Regardless, in a second or two, she clicked accept and the Insta-stalking began. It felt like she was seeing the life of a known-stranger. Someone whose heart she knew, despite their short interaction, but whose life, she was now privy to, through photos. It was exhilarating!

But what came next, led to even more 'fluttering dragons in the tummy'- one hour after she accepted his follow request and followed him back, Arjun sent her a direct message, despite the time difference and it being around six in the morning, NYC time.

He wrote:

"Hi Nadia, I'm so glad I found you. Luckily Nadia from BCU was rare enough. Can we talk once you wake up? Here is my number- (646) 371 7324. Please text or call me.

Ps: I haven't seen you at the East End Park all Fall. Don't like leaf peeping?"

So Arjun assumed she was still in NYC and had been looking out for her on his jogs. The dragons were now taking roller coaster rides in her belly, and Nadia hadn't realised it but she was grinning like a teenager who saw Justin Beiber's Calvin Klein underwear ad for the first time.

Nadia didn't call, (international charges and nervousness stopped her) but she replied to the message on Instagram immediately:

"Hi Arjun,

I'm glad you found me too. Are you kidding? Red is my favourite colour and Fall is my second favourite season. I love leaf peeping! But I'm not in NYC anymore. I have, for the time being at least, moved back to India. Had some loose heartstrings to tie up, if you know what I mean.

What did you want to talk about? I can't call but I can Facetime. +91 9819450700

PS: Good to know you are jogging again!"

Arjun replied within eight minutes. Wow, this guy was on social media a lot! Or he was eager to hear from Nadia.

"Is my time, 11 pm okay? That is India time- 8:30 am. I'm just heading to work now or I would've Facetimed you sooner. Good to know the heartstrings are being tied up:)"

"8:30 am works. And how is Rebecca by the way?" Nadia replied. She knew it was pretty direct, but she just had to know!!! She couldn't wait over twelve hours to find out if Arjun was single or not.

Arjun replied in three minutes this time:

"We broke up two months back. I ended it. I'm trying to tie up some heartstrings of my own and needed to find you."

And then one minute later, he messaged again:

"Are you seeing someone?"

"Nope" was Nadia's one word reply, while her heart thumped wildly in her chest. How would she sleep that night? How would she wait over twelve hours to talk to Arjun? What did he want to say? And she was in India now, a continent away. What did all of this mean?

But suddenly, her heart reminded her of Susan's words from that morning, "I see love coming your way very soon... you have met already. It is an old, old bond. Lifetimes probably."

WHAT THE HELL!!!!!!!!

Is Arjun my... No... I can't even bare to think it yet. It's too soon and too early and too uncertain and he is tooooo far away. Chillll Nadia.

But... could he be... was it too preposterous to even think?

Was her gut playing tricks on her? Was her heart jumping the gun and all sense of logic, as well?

It was CRAZY to think that a guy she met months ago, just twice, and who now lived thousands of miles away from her, could be... the one.

Calm down Nadia, she reminded herself, *Baby steps.*

G loved this part. In every lifetime that Arjun and Nadia shared, G loved watching the two of them find each other. Even God has a mushy side, you know.

The helper and G had been deprived of this mushy pleasure the last time.

Married to Zaal = no Arjun. Nadia and Arjun had never met again. That path had been left un-taken.

***

Since her entire world seemed to be suspended in anticipation of the call with Arjun, Nadia decided to distract herself a little. She went over the list of un-answered questions from the tarot that morning. On re-reading it, Nadia realised that she does indeed have one creative skill- writing. She had never pursued it professionally and had never even taken a single writing course in college, but Nadia had always written poetry. She had never considered it a skill or talent, because she had never shared her poetry with anyone. Ever!

It was her little secret.

Like the memory of Chris now did, her poetry had always lived inside her heart, unspoken, never to be revealed or shown to anyone. It was just tooo personal. It was her escape.

How can I let someone read my escape?

Nonetheless, it was a creative skill, and Nadia would give it more thought later, she promised herself.

After a night of tossing and turning, getting out of bed at 5:15 am and making a ginormous breakfast for Dad and herself – Omelettes and bacon with whole wheat toast and marmalade, she retreated into the guest room at Dad's house, for her much awaited, facetime with Arjun.

At 8:25 am, Arjun called. It felt surreal to see his name flash on her phone screen for the first time. Immediately, Nadia picked up the voice call. Clearly, neither of them was trying to 'play it cool' at all.

"Hi," she said excited to hear his voice again after all these months.

"Hi," he answered, sounding shy.

"How have you been, Arjun?" Nadia asked, genuinely wanting to know.

"I've had a few months of soul searching, honestly. I broke up with Rebecca. And…and I keep thinking about you."

"Sorry about your breakup. Are you doing okay?" the dragons were back in her belly, and this time they were tap dancing.

Did he just say he's been thinking of ME??

"Yeah yeah. It was a long time coming. I just needed to do the right thing, you know." How well Nadia understood that.

"Listen, so how come you moved back to India? How are you?" he asked, the disappointment apparent in his voice. Talk about bad timing.

"I moved back to figure out my next step. I realised that I had a lot of healing to do and it has ended up being a great thing. I'm actually getting to work on my relationship with my parents. It wasn't the best, growing up. But I do miss NYC in the Fall."

"Fall will be there again next year. But you got to do what you got to do…. I keep thinking that I need to have a heart to heart with my dad but I still haven't gotten around to it." Arjun responded. He understood the importance of 'mending bridges'.

"Where in India are you by the way?" He continued, before Nadia could ask him more about his dad.

"Oh I'm in Goa. My dad moved here earlier this year. But I grew up in Mumbai."

"Yea you told me over Nachos, remember? I told you that my sister now lives in Mumbai and I used to visit Mumbai a lot for swimming competitions as a kid."

"Of course I remember. You told me you grew up in Pune and I said, 'It's okay, no one is perfect'!"

They laughed once again at this joke from several months ago, alluding to how Pune city was a less-cool, much smaller version of Mumbai.

His laugh sounds sooo good. If only I could see his dimples.

"Umm... should we video chat?" Nadia asked, summoning her bravery.

"Yes!" Arjun agreed immediately, turning his camera on as Nadia did the same.

Ahhhh......There he is!

Sitting on his bed in a white T-shirt and wet hair, he smiled a huge smile. And there were those dimples! Is it possible to see someone's eyes twinkle through Facetime?

Nadia was in her PJs too, an old red BCU T-shirt and shorts, her hair was up in a bun, but who cares. She got to see those dimples.

"Hi," Arjun said again and then asked "Soooo when can I see you, in real life? Please tell me you are coming back soon?"

"I don't know... I haven't even figured out my next step. Honestly, since I moved back here, I don't have a concrete plan. I'm just waiting."

"Waiting for?"

Nadia didn't know exactly how to complete that sentence yet.

"Well… I guess waiting to figure out my calling. I worked at eWay after college, but I'm sure that marketing isn't it."

"Hmmm so what is your dream? Any options so far?"

"Okay promise you won't laugh?

"I may. But tell me anyway." And she did. It felt so easy to talk to him. His eyes had an earnest quality that drew her in.

"I went for a tarot session yesterday, and the lady told me I should do something creative and I will know very soon what that something is… and then last night I sort of realised, and you are the first person I'm telling this to… that I write. Poetry mostly. But I've never shown it to anyone or even thought about it much. Maybe, writing is what the tarot lady was talking about?"

"That is definitely food for thought," Arjun replied, stealing the phrase from her mind.

Now it was Nadia's turn to chuckle when Arjun unknowingly referred to the title of Nadia's Tarot 'mull points' list, "Yes. That's exactly what it is!"

He didn't understand why she had giggled, but he didn't mind. It felt good to just talk to her. Is it possible to miss someone you barely know?

"I'm stoked to be the first one you've told. Your secret is safe with me. Though…why haven't you ever shown your poems to anyone?"

"I'm a shy person," Nadia admitted. "And my writing is extremely personal. I feel... naked, if I even think of showing them to anyone."

"But it can also be liberating."

"More food for thought," She agreed.

"I'm going to mull over this," Nadia went on, "Maybe there is a reason God gave me this skill."

They spoke and looked at each other for over two hours, that first time. He told her all about the drama at work after his break up with Rebecca. Working with your ex is something no one should have to go through. Eeks!

He told her about the heart to heart he wants to have with his dad about how it is apparent that his dad is depressed and needs to get help for it. But such conversations take an immense courage he hadn't found yet. 'Baby steps' Nadia had told him and he felt a little better about his procrastination. Finally they hung up when Arjun had to go to sleep. Time difference can be a ginormous pain in the ass!

After months of turmoil and tough decisions though, Arjun slept like a baby that night. He was glad he had been brave enough to find and reach out to Nadia.

Despite the bad timing and the fact that Nadia was in Goa, not Manhattan anymore, he felt a connection. He felt hopeful.

She felt the same way – connected, hopeful and... grateful.

G, thank you for this. Even if it doesn't go anywhere, thank you! Nadia thought, on hanging up with Arjun. The dragons were now playing Frisbee right behind her belly button.

CHAPTER 18

REVELATION

The next night, before going to bed, Nadia started making a list of all the people in her life she was grateful for, the ones she had learnt from, the ones she loves. The usual suspects were on the list of course – her family, Chris, friends, professors from university, old colleagues at eWay, Gabby, Isla, Tara and gradually, Nadia went further back into her childhood.

She used to come home and watch Oprah every day after school while eating lunch, so Goddess O went on the list. Mom and Dad used to be at work and Nadia would be home alone with Gulabo all day, till they returned around six or seven each evening. Gulabo had been her nanny from ages six to sixteen. She was a loving, loud, orthodox Catholic, thin as a wire lady, who had practically raised Nadia.

When Nadia had exams, Gulabo would fast, to ask God to help Nadia do well. When Nadia was ill, she would push Mom to take her to the doctor, sooner rather than later, and then fast, to ask God to get Nadia well again. When Nadia got ill-treated in High school, Gulabo fasted to ask God to end Nadia's mean-girl problems and even got her prayer group to pray for Nadia's final exam results.

And the best part about Gulabo was, despite all her fasting, she cooked food that could turn your life upside down! Her meals were enough to lift Nadia's spirits on many a gloomy teenage day. She was the one who had instilled in Nadia, a love for cooking and food. They still spoke on the phone every other month or so and Nadia visited Gulabo whenever she was in Mumbai. Gulabo was currently doing a weekly fast to ask God to help Nadia find a 'good job'. Gulabo had retired when she turned seventy and Nadia turned sixteen, just after Nadia and Roxanne had moved out of Dad's house.

Gulabo had been the saffron flavouring to Nadia's unappetising childhood, and she was supremely grateful for Gulabo's constant love, care and food.

When Facetiming with Arjun the following morning (yes, they would do this every day now), Nadia told him about Gulabo.

"You know nobody can make Biryani like Gulabo. Come to think of it, I should ask her for the recipe."

"How old is she now?"

"Must be almost eighty by now I think." And that's when it hit Nadia. Gulabo probably wouldn't be around for much longer.

Picking up on her thought, Arjun said "You should write down her recipes, preserve a little piece of Gulabo forever."

"Yeah I should…That's a brilliant idea! Although, I can't bear to think about a world without Gulabo fasting in it," Nadia said, already getting a little blue thinking about Gulabo's mortality.

"I've learned a lot from her over the years," Nadia went on, "and so many of my childhood memories are tied to food, because of her."

"You really do love food, don't you?" Arjun questioned, "even when we met, you almost immediately spoke about Nachos!"

They laughed at this, and nothing could be more true, Nadia realised. Food and cooking were very important to her. They was inextricably linked to most of her memories.

Chicken wings= Chris

Nachos= Boston

Biryani= Gulabo

Pea soup= Gulabo's fast-breaking meal of choice

Pancakes and/or chicken noodle soup= comfort meal after any and all problems

Kheer= Sabina Granny

Tacos= Tara and Isla

And now, pork vindaloo= Goan sunsets and the sea

Nadia loved food so much, she could write a book about it!

Wait..........

That's it!!!! A book about cooking.

Arjun could see the churnings of Nadia's mind on her face, and asked "What's the eureka moment Dee?"(He had started calling her Dee in their second Facetime conversation, for no apparent reason. Dee came from the second syllable of her name 'Naa-**Dee**-Yaah'. And Nadia loved it.)

"Arjun…I think I just figured out my next step." His face instantly lit up on hearing this.

"A recipe book!" Nadia continued, "But more than a basic recipe book…Mmm like a compilation of my most important memories and all the food associated with them."

"I LOVE this idea," he exclaimed, practically clapping. His dimples looked half an inch deeper now.

"And guess what I'll call it," Nadia went on, as the ideas rushed into her head like a torrential downpour.

"What??"

"Food for Thought."

***

Reverberating in my mind

By Nadia

My name sounds so sweet on your lips.
I want to hear it again and again.
Dee
Dee
I want to hear the tenderness,
The care,
The want,
The thirst.
I want to hear you say my name,
Like nobody else ever does.
As if calling out for a drop of warmth
On a blizzard afternoon.
As if calling out to an ocean breeze
For a barren heart.
As if Nadia, isn't just my name,
But who I am.

And you get it.
***

The next day, Nadia went up to Akbar while he was having his afternoon tea and reading the newspaper, all excited to tell him about her book idea.

"Dad, I have some exciting news to share with you. You remember Gulabo?"

Looking up from his paper Dad replied, "Of course, what's the news?".

Almost jumping with glee, Nadia spat out her plan, "I have decided to write a cook-book, with Gulabo's recipes and other recipes connected to my life. Like a memory cum recipe book. I've already spoken to Gulabo, and she is on-board. I'm calling it 'Food for Thought'."

Dad looked confused for a minute, and then simply said, "Follow your heart Nadia," with a smile.

WHAAAT?

Was Akbar…her father…saying this?? Nadia was dumbfounded.

Who is this man and what has he done with my father.

She could tell that Goa had done Dad good, and he was way more open now. But 'follow your heart'? What happened to 'follow the money', or 'everyone has problems' or 'choose a respectable profession'? These were the maxims she had heard from dad while growing up.

Of course, she liked 'follow your heart' much better.

Swallowing her happy disbelief, Nadia replied, "Thanks dad. That is very sweet of you to say." Dad smiled and went back to his tea and *Economic Times*.

Nadia had come to Goa to mend fences with her father and have honest conversations with him. As she sat there, watching the new Akbar sip his tea, Nadia suddenly decided to go for it.

"Dad. You have changed a lot…in a good way. Any particular reason though? You seem much happier."

Dad looked up slowly, seeming a little scared. As if he didn't want Nadia to notice that he was… happy.

"Changed? Maybe it's just the retirement. And Goa."

"Could be…" Nadia went on, "But I just want you to know that I'm happy, that you're happy."

"I am happy. Thank you Nadia. I should've moved here years ago. But I didn't. I have… friends here," Dad said. But there was something in the way he said 'friends'. It seemed… odd. As if he wasn't trying to say 'friends' at all. As if he was…could it be that dad was *with* someone? Dating, perhaps?

What else can make someone change so much, if not love, Nadia thought, remembering the 'Strength' card.

The idea of Dad dating, pleased Nadia.

Wow! Major progress! Dad has let someone in?!

She decided to probe a little further.

"Who is your *best* friend here, Dad?" she asked, stressing on best, but very subtly.

Dad looked shy all of a sudden, and a slight red tinge, coloured his cheeks, "Oh, no one in particular. Just… friends, you know."

This confirmed it. Dad was hiding something. His face was giving away what his words were trying to disguise.

"Okay. As I said, I'm happy you're happy." And Nadia dropped it. She didn't need to know more until dad was ready to tell her.

Soooooo exciting.

Everyone should have love, right G? Nadia thought.

"Yes, everyone should let themselves love," God replied, for he knew, what Nadia didn't yet.

Akbar had taken a lifetime to learn this lesson. But learn it, he had.

CHAPTER 19

TRUTH TIME

A week later, Nadia was busily working on her recipe cum memory book, when Dad came into the room. She was in full blown nerd mode and didn't notice him.

"Nadia," he said, approaching her from behind.

"Oh!" She jumped, "You scared me."

And then she saw it. Dad looked perfectly petrified. He was actually, physically sweating. It was December in Goa, which means there was no weather-related reason to sweat.

"What's up, Dad?" Nadia asked, concerned.

"I want you to meet someone. A friend of mine," Dad said with his hands firmly attached to his sides.

"Oh okay!" Nadia replied, bewildered, wondering why Akbar looked so nervous.

As soon as Nadia said okay, a man entered the room from behind Akbar.

He had a big smile on his face and said, "Hi Nadia, your dad has told me so much about you. I'm Rudy."

"Hi Rudy," Nadia replied, still confused by this sudden encounter and her dad's reaction to it.

"Sorry my room's such a mess. Dad usually likes a very clean house," she said with a smile.

"Oh yes. I know all about your dad's neatness habit," Rudy said with a warm smile and what looked like affection.

As Nadia explained her book idea to Rudy, who asked about what she was up to, she took Rudy's physical appearance in. He was a short, stout, British man with greying hair, small beady eyes and a happy face. He was wearing a blue and orange Hawaiian shirt and Bermuda shorts. He hadn't once stopped smiling since he entered Nadia's room, and she could tell that it was sincere. He was sincerely happy to be there, with Nadia and Dad, in her room, talking about her book.

Who is this guy? How come Dad has never mentioned him before? How come he suddenly burst into my room? And why does Dad still have a constipated look on his face?

Rudy began to talk about how he had been a lawyer in London and had retired to Goa a couple of years back. He then looked over at Akbar and said "And it is the best decision I ever made," with an unmistakeable look in his eyes – love.

Slowly, like a drop of water trickling through a thin piece of paper, realisation, seeped into Nadia.

Rudy was Dad's 'friend'. The reason he was different. The reason he was happy.

Suddenly Nadia's tummy felt queasy and her toes and fingers grew glacier cold

Oh man! Is this really happening.

"Rudy… Dad," she suddenly said standing up, "Excuse me. I need to use the loo. I'll be back in just a minute."

"Sure," Rudy said, still smiling. He looked at Dad, as if he were willing him to smile as well. But Akbar's face stayed in a twisted look of sweaty dread.

Nadia rushed into the bathroom and locked the door. Turning around slowly, she looked into the mirror, into her own eyes.

Am I going crazy?

Or did I just see what I think I saw… are Rudy and Dad… together? Is dad….gay?

G… help!!

A blanketing sense of calm engulfed Nadia. Her eyes teared up a little and let out a single tear as she tried to breathe slowly and calm her heart, looking down at the sink now. It suddenly all made sense. S-h-o-c-k-i-n-g as it was, it made sense.

Nadia's heart began to return to a stable rhythm. Her toes and fingers remained icicle-like though.

She took three deep breaths and unlocked the door ready to face the truth.

As soon as she opened the door, Dad and Rudy looked at her, trying to size-up her reaction.

Nadia looked Akbar dead in the eyes, and said "Dad, I'm so happy to meet Rudy... Thank you!"

Akbar blinked – like his worst fear had been realised, but it had been utterly anti-climactic. You could actually see him exhale his anxiety, as he turned to Rudy.

Then Nadia looked at Rudy and said, "I hope to get to know you better over time, Rudy."

"Me too, Nadia," he replied. This had been music to Rudy's happy, sun-burned ears.

***

Over the next few days, Nadia wondered whether or not to talk to Dad about it. She didn't want to push him too much or make him even more uncomfortable than he already was. But she didn't want him to feel like she didn't approve either.

To Nadia, love was just love. It didn't matter what the label was, or the gender, or what society felt about it. Dad was happy and she was happy for him. Nothing could be simpler.

Everyone should have love.

She now recalled the times in the distant past, when Dad had said or implied something homophobic, and Nadia wished she had expressed her feelings on this topic to him, years ago. But how could she have known...

Eventually, she decided to let Akbar take the lead on this one. Hopefully, he knew that she knew. And now, he knew that she was okay with it. The ball was in his court. He could play… or not.

No wonder Dad had always shut her out. No wonder Dad always felt closed off and distant.

Poor guy has been running from himself allll these years.

He hadn't resented Nadia, as she thought he did all along, but just wanted the freedom to be who he was.

Growing up in India in the early 1960s when Akbar was a child, you were taught unequivocally that – love, sex and marriage are only for husband and wife. No other permutation and combination is allowed. No other combination is holy. All other combinations were illegal.

Section 377 of the 'Indian Penal Code' stated (Thank heavens this colonial era law was repealed on 6th September, 2018) :

"Unnatural offences: Whoever voluntarily has carnal intercourse against the order of nature with any man, woman or animal shall be punished with imprisonment for life, or with imprisonment of either description for term which may extend to ten years, and shall also be liable to fine."

Against the order of nature????????

No wonder Akbar had let the tide of societal pressure lead him into a life, he didn't really want. What was the other option? Imprisonment!

So instead of being imprisoned in an Indian jail, he had imprisoned himself in a jail of his own making, shutting real love and truth out. It was safer that way.

It all makes sense now. Finally, I have the whole story.

***

377 Reasons to Hide

By Nadia

You can tell me your secrets.
Come out to play!
You are safe with me.
It's a brand-new day.

No point in hiding.
Nobody will go seek.
No point in playing
This game of chor-police.
Times have changed now,
Nobody will mind.
No need to fear
Being caught, or left behind.

You are safe with me now.
Your secret is safe!
But sounder than hiding,
Is to let the love-police
See your face.

I'll help you be free,
If that is your choice.
Nobody will leave you.
Come, play the game. Use your voice!

***

"You know, in all of this, I feel the worst for Mom," Nadia confessed over Facetime, as she told Arjun about what she had come to know the day before. It felt completely easy and natural to tell Arjun just about anything. Nothing was taboo. Nothing felt off limits. For once, Nadia was able to be an open book.

"Yeah me too," he admitted. "Being lied to like that for decades. Will you tell your Mom about Rudy?"

"No way! This is Dad's story to tell or not tell. I'm not even going to tell Sabina Granny."

"Just me?" Arjun asked with a grin.

"Just you," Nadia confirmed in a softer voice. She had only wanted to talk to Arjun about this. She had only told Arjun about her Mom's diary, Dad's Rudy, the conversation she had with Sabina Granny the night before she had begun her closet cleaning expedition, and many, many other things.

And Arjun had told Nadia about his family's financial problems. His childhood and constantly difficult relationship with his father, and even how he had thought about Nadia every day since the day they met in the park that spring.

He was an open book. He let her read his happy and not so happy chapters, without hesitation.

"Dee…" Arjun said, making the dragons flutter. He suddenly sounded desperate, "I need to see you. For real. Facetime just doesn't cut it. I can't kiss you through facetime."

And with that, the dragons went berserk. They were jumping on the trampoline of her diaphragm. Arjun had just said kiss. He wanted to kiss her.

She thought about it at least 33.75 times a day, but he had said it.

"I want that too," she replied, in a softer voice.

"But I got to finish the cookbook first. I have meetings lined up with three literary agents in Mumbai next month. I've already been rejected by two agents."

"I know," he sighed, "okkaaayy…you do you. I'll just have to be content with seeing and talking to you through my phone for now."

"How PG 13 of us, right?"

"Haha totally! Just like high school…" Arjun replied.

And so, their high school meets adult life romance continued, while Nadia left Goa and moved back to Mumbai to be closer to Gulabo and the publishing world, while finishing up the book.

Once in Mumbai, Nadia spent every day writing, cooking with Gulabo to experiment with various versions of recipes, Facetiming with Arjun and day dreaming about seeing Arjun again.

Nadia's life felt more open now, like love was rushing in at every corner and there was just no room for any darkness. It was all light and song. She believed in her anthem more and more, over the next month, for hadn't her life led her here?

Tra la la la la la la I can do anything. Anything at all.

Wow la la la la la la I can do anything. Anything at all.

Dum da dum dee dum da dee,

I can be, I can be,

Anything. Anything at all

I can have anything tra la la la la la la

Absolutely anything wow la la la la la la

I'm sure.

G just sat back with an immensely content look. All was well with the Reset.

CHAPTER 20

SPIRALLING

For two months, Nadia lived in Mumbai, finishing up the edits of her book. She lived with Sabina Granny and visited different publishers and agents almost every day, to make sure her first book found a publisher. She had to answer her calling, with her best!

Finally, when she got accepted after nineteen rejections, it felt almost dreamlike. She had decided to self-publish and was researching options online when she got that one email she had been waiting for; the one saying 'The Red Box Publishing House' would be interested to meet and acquire the rights to this manuscript.

I did it! I did it! I did it!!

Soon, it came time to design a cover for the book, she considered putting a photo of Gulabo on it, to pay homage to the key contributor of the recipes. She had gotten some important Mexican recipes from Chris's mother as well and had even emailed 'Nacho Mamas' in Boston. They had obliged and were featured in Nadia's book too, because they had brought about her first 'pseudo-date' with Arjun.

Gulabo, however, was shy and didn't want her face or name on any cover (she had even denied the royalty split, but Nadia had insisted on that). So Nadia had to continue brainstorming. She spoke to her mother, father, Rudy, Sabina Granny, Gabby, Isla, Tara and took all their advice that ranged from practical and imaginative, to down-right bizarre.

Sabina Granny actually suggested putting a picture of Nadia eating an air bubble made out of candy floss on the cover, to show that she was literally eating thoughts!!! Naturally, Nadia had to veto that gem.

Arjun didn't give any suggestions; he wanted Nadia to "find the right answer". He kept saying "Baby, you will know when you know. Just like I knew with you."

Awwwwww.

Two and a half months of waiting to see Nadia had turned him into quite the mush-monster. He would send Nadia pictures of himself jogging in different parts of Manhattan to show her where he wanted to take her once they were together. He would send her gifts with his sister who lived in Mumbai, every two weeks or so. Once, it was a snow globe with a cherry blossom tree in it. Another time, he mailed her a bottle of Sriracha Sauce, since Nadia had been complaining about not being able to find Sriracha in Mumbai. His gifts were always thoughtful and made Nadia miss him desperately. But she had a calling to answer first.

On the 14th of February, Arjun got flowers delivered to Nadia's home in Mumbai – seventy six red roses. One for each day they had spoken on Facetime, since they had reconnected. If this had been anyone else, Nadia may have hurled from the cheesiness-quotient. But it was Arjun. And it was love. And they were red roses.

She came home from the editor that day to see the living room filled with the roses and lunch ready on the table. Granny was waiting to eat with Nadia and had cooked Gulabo's famously decadent Biryani that day. The aroma of the roses and Biryani did something to Nadia, and she just instantly knew- This was her cover page!

"Granny this is it! This is what I want for my cover. Roses and Biryani. It's simple and yet beautiful. Look how well all the colours on this dining table are playing off of each other. It's a visual treat."

Granny chuckled and said, "Yes, good idea. Roses for rose."

"What?" Nadia asked, confused for a millisecond. But then, suddenly, she understood the joke.

How could I not have got this before? It's so obvious!

Gulabo means 'Rose' in Hindi!

The answer had been under her long nose, all along. It was the perfect tribute to Gulabo. The tarot reader, had predicted it and once again hit the nail on Nadia's, now swirling, head.

Oh G, you genius! Nadia said as she began her lunch.

"Remember how Nadia didn't eat biryani for three years when she and Zaal went off rice the last time," The helper said.

220

"Zaal and his pursuit of the perfect body!" G sighed, recalling the pre Reset life that had been filled with so many missed joys. But not this time.

***

On the morning of 22nd February, Nadia woke up bright and early to write. Ever since she was young, she always liked the early morning hours to get work done. The months leading up to her 12th grade finals and then the SATs, she had made it a habit to wake up at 5 am to study. Mom was asleep at 5 am. The house was quiet. Nobody would nag her, she could make herself a chai in peace, and she could watch the bright green parakeets with their lipstick red beaks outside her window. They sat in the gulmohar tree beyond her study desk and began to cheep-cheep at around 6 am. This way she would get a few good solitary study hours before the apartment and street below were bustling with the hum of wakening life.

On that morning, she was having a hard time picking out the memories to include in the last three chapters of her cookbook. The cheep-cheeping helped and after brainstorming for an hour or so, she was able to finalise the memory to include in chapter eleven, the third from last chapter of the book.

It would contain the story of the day Dad, Rudy and she had dined together for the first time in Goa nearly two months ago. Rudy had cooked an amazing pork vindaloo that night, a recipe he had gotten right after years of experimenting, he said. That was the first time Nadia had seen Dad begin to chill out and smile when he was around both Nadia and Rudy. He even sat on the same side as Rudy and let Rudy call him 'darling' in front of his daughter.

Rudy must be quite the magician to tunnel in with Dad the way he had.

While writing the memory, Nadia of course was careful to cleverly veil Rudy and Dad's relationship, calling them pals. It is India after all!

But even for other reasons, this memory had been a hard one for Nadia to write about. The truth was, while she was happy that her father had at last been honest with himself and her, Nadia now found herself beginning to resent him for all those years where he hadn't – the years of dishonesty.

She had easily accepted his truth that day, when he came out to her. Love is love. Simple. But what wasn't *simple* for Nadia to deal with… had crept up on her, slowly, over the following weeks.

G why am I feeling this way? Nadia wondered, frustrated. *Why can't emotions go in a straight line, from one to the next to the next.*

But always the artist, G had designed it to be like a spiral. Sometimes you think you have gotten past something, but a month later you are right back to loop one. Nadia's initial relief and sense of clarity had, over the months, given way to a niggling resentment and anger.

Of late, she would lie in bed at night, with a clenched jaw, angry at Akbar for not having had the courage to be himself sooner. She was angry at him for marrying Roxanne. She was angry at him for having a child he didn't want. She was angry at him for keeping her at arm's length for twenty seven years. Most of all, she was angry at him for being afraid all those years. And she worried whether that lack of courage, was in her too.

She felt guilty about feeling this way, and the tussle between mature Nadia and not-wanting-to-be-so-mature Nadia, went on in her mind and heart. She felt guilty about being angry at Akbar for she knew how hard it must have been for him to hide himself for most of his life.

It was sad really! An impossible situation. He was doing the best he could, Mature Nadia would say to convince the other part of herself.

But still, she couldn't help but feel…cheated. She felt like she had been tricked into being a part of this lie; This cover–up story where Akbar pretended to be straight, and married. The lie where Roxanne pretended to be the doting and selfless Mother of the Millennium; And Nadia pretended to be okay with it all.

It's not easy to get over twenty seven years' worth of lies and Nadia was struggling with the spiral.

Why me? she asked G, *why couldn't I have had two parents who wanted and cared for me, the way most people do.*

Why couldn't I have had it simple?

God let her sit with this disequilibrium though, for he knew its importance. Sometimes it may seem like a step back, but the spiral, if done right, could lead to three steps forward; the snakes and ladders game of life.

Anger, was Nadia's unwelcome houseguest. She only wanted to allow compassion in; Compassion is a good emotion, she knew. Anger is bad emotion, she thought. Because for her, most things were bad or good. Black or white. And Nadia had always struggled with the spectrum of grey emotions.

Just like she had always struggled with being honest about how she really felt. Given a choice to be honest, or be liked, Nadia would chose the latter, ten out of ten times.

True or false:-

Isn't our well-being dependant on being liked?

Isn't too much honesty un-likeable?

She hadn't spoken her mind years ago when Akbar showed his homophobia when speaking of Chris. She hadn't clearly shown her pain at the way she had been brought up, to her parents. She hadn't shown Akbar or Roxanne, how she really felt about anything she thought they would disagree with. Therefore, without realising it, Nadia had, all her life, done exactly what her parents had – hidden in plain sight.

And so the family pattern would have gone on and on, ad infinitum, had G not intervened.

***

On 22nd February at 9 am, Nadia decided to take a break from writing and have breakfast, which she ate every morning with Sabina Granny. She left her laptop, got up from her writing desk and walked into the kitchen. The cook, Aisha, was already making lunch-chicken farchas, but Granny wasn't around.

"Hi Aisha, where's Granny?" Nadia asked in Hindi, as she entered the kitchen.

"I haven't seen her all morning. She must be sleeping-in today."

"Please go wake her up na," Nadia said, taking a bite out of an apple she had just pulled out of the fridge.

"I'm starving! We should eat breakfast soon."

Aisha left the kitchen to go wake up Sabina, and within a few seconds, Nadia heard her scream. She dropped the apple and ran into Sabina Granny's bedroom to find Aisha trying to pick up Granny, who was lying on the floor, awake, but unresponsive.

At first, Nadia thought she had just had a fall, but then, on trying to pick up Sabina, she realised something was wrong. Granny seemed…stuck, like a statue. The two of them just about managed to pick her up and half-drag her into bed. Nadia was sweating with fear by then and called their family doctor who said he was rushing over and calling an ambulance too. Then, she called Akbar, who became hysterical and finally stammered out that he would catch the next flight home.

All the while, Nadia kept her hand on Sabina's chest to make sure her heart was still beating. It was.

The words to long forgotten prayers unexpectedly reached Nadia's lips and she began praying under her breath. She wasn't a religious person at all, and she usually never prayed. "*What's the point of reciting verses in a language I don't understand, when G and I can communicate in any language and with our own words,*" she believed. But that day, while they waited for the doctor and the ambulance, she prayed.

Aisha called up Roxanne, who left work and rushed over. Nadia could not have been more grateful for her mother, than she was that day. Roxanne had seen her own mother and father grow old and fall sick, and she knew how to handle these situations, which helped Nadia's heartbeat ease up a little. The doctor was sure it was a stroke, and they quickly rushed Sabina to the best hospital in town.

But all the while, Granny didn't speak, or even move much. She was alive, but unlike herself. She wasn't the spunky, independent lady Nadia knew. She was terrified and…stiff.

When Akbar arrived a few hours later, he was overflowing with fear. Even in his late 50's, losing his mother was unimaginable for him. He seemed like a child; vulnerable and needing care. Nadia tried to allay his fears and held his hand when he entered Sabina's room and saw his mother like that for the first time, but she couldn't battle the truth – a stroke is a big freaking deal.

While Akbar was speaking to the doctors, Nadia broke away for some time and called Rudy. He promised to come to Mumbai if things got worse. Akbar hadn't wanted Rudy there because Roxanne, Sabina & his entire Mumbai world didn't know, and he wanted to keep it that way. Akbar wanted to keep his image intact and not rock the boat, Rudy said. Nadia understood.

Then Nadia called Arjun. It was 5:30 am New York time, but she just couldn't wait any longer. They had texted through the day, but Nadia hadn't had the time to call. As soon as Arjun picked up, Nadia started to cry. However, the gush of emotion, passed, just as suddenly as it had begun. She had needed that vent and now that it was out of the way, they could talk.

"How is your Granny doing Dee?" he asked, with concern in his soft voice.

"We don't really know yet. The doctors say they won't know the extent of the damage to her brain until she is stabilised and off sedation. I'm just scared. "

"You told me she is a fighter. She will get better," Arjun said trying to reassure her, probably wishing he could've been there with her that day.

"Was it this scary for you when your father had a stroke?"

Arjun had told her about his father's stroke five years back, and how he was doing much better now after physical therapy and years to heal.

"It was really bad because I was in New York and being far away made it very hard for me. I rushed back, but those twenty two hours on that plane, were the worst of my life so far."

He continued, "But the doctors treated him very quickly, and that helped him a great deal."

"That's just the thing. I don't know how long Granny was lying on the floor like that. We found her at nine. But I don't know when she had the stroke. What if we were too late?"

With that, tears once again filled Nadia's eyes. "I love her so much," she sobbed into the phone. "I just want her to be okay. She looks like she is in pain, Arjun."

Nadia was blubbering and sniffling and there was nothing anyone could say to calm her fears. So Arjun let her cry. And when she was done, Nadia said, "Okay. I'm going to go back now. Sit with mom and dad. Sorry for waking you up."

"Any time, Dee. And just keep reminding yourself that you can do this! You are strong."

She smiled a small smile, "Yes. I am. I will do that. Bye baby."

"Bye dee. Miss you."

Nadia knew she was strong, and this too would pass.

Shit happens. Shit will pass, she told herself after hanging up, which made her chuckle.

CHAPTER 21

RECYCLE

Exactly a month from the day she had the stroke, Sabina Granny passed on. Even though the doctors had said that she had very little time left, and Nadia had known it was coming, the wave of grief was strong and excruciating.

It had been emotionally strenuous, watching Sabina wither away day by day in the hospital bed. But it had given them all time to prepare for the inevitable. And for that, Nadia was grateful.

Nadia was also grateful for the deepened bond with Granny that those last few months of living in India had given her. What a shame it would have been if Sabina had passed before Nadia had moved back home. She thanked G for that big mercy!

"She missed out on this the last time," The helper remarked as they watched her say goodbye to Sabina this time.

"Only adding to her regrets," G said.

She had been in NYC with Zaal, still at her eWay job when Sabina had passed on.

But still, it wasn't enough. She wanted more time with her grandmother. And sadness filled her, every time she remembered that she couldn't have any more of it. She would never again eat breakfast with Granny, or come home to Granny cutting up the day's newspaper, or have a laugh with this person that she had always loved, but had gotten to know much better in the last few months.

In two days, they were having a memorial service for her, because Sabina had explicitly stated time and time again over the years, that she didn't want any religious service- 'no muss-fuss', as she had called it. So it would be just a gathering of friends and family, where they would speak about Sabina and honour her memory.

While trying to write a speech for Granny, Nadia realised that there would be some people present at the memorial service who didn't even like Sabina. Many relatives had detested Sabina's outspoken nature, and direct, often rude remarks.

Yet, Sabina had lived life on her own terms, unapologetic; and that was what Nadia admired most about her Granny – she was a renegade. She never shrouded even her worst emotions. Whenever Sabina had been upset, angry, sad or irritated, everyone had known it. And most people had actually come to accept that about Sabina.

It was just who she was.

Nadia recalled the time when Sabina and Roxanne had had a fighting match over a family dinner one night when Nadia was eight or nine, where Sabina had bluntly said, "Roxanne dear, you just want to be angry, so you are.

And that is your choice, but I'm bloody well not going to take it or give you the sympathy you so constantly crave."

Stunned, Roxanne hadn't known how to respond to that declaration. But true to her words, Sabina didn't take it, ever! She was never a martyr. And despite that, or maybe because of it, Roxanne had been at Sabina's death bed. For you can't help but respect someone who sparred with you, openly and outspokenly.

Respect is a funny thing, Nadia thought as she pondered how as a child, she never wanted to be respected, because, well, she was a kid.

Kids don't care about respect. But now as an adult, it's a different story.

Nadia knew that like most people, she too, had grown up wanting to fit in and be liked. And unknowingly, she had adapted her actions and personality to what she perceived as likeable and acceptable.

But then, does cultivating likeability, kill who you really are?

Granny had practised the answer all her life, hadn't she? And then the speech practically wrote itself.

Sabina's honesty with Nadia that night in Mumbai when she confessed her short-comings as a mother to her grand-daughter, was not something most people could or would do. But Sabina had.

Telling staunchly religious members of her extended family, that she didn't believe in their 'claims' of heaven and hell, and their version of morality, did not win Sabina many fans. But she did it anyway.

She may have often seemed brutal, or too much, or not nice, but she spoke her truth anyway. It was the way she was. And like it or not, that was how she stayed.

Only Sabina's opinion mattered to Sabina. And most people, in time, grew to accept and admire that about her.

Nadia saw it now, clear as day — Sabina's well-being hadn't depended on being liked. It had depended on being honest to herself. Honesty had set Sabina free.

I want that. I want to be like that.

Honesty Is The Best Policy
By Nadia

Honesty is the best policy, they say.
But they only speak.
They never do.

Honesty will get you in trouble,
I had learned.
And trouble must be avoided,
Just like the truth.
Honesty leaves you raw,
They preach.
Better to shield it away,
Pretend, till your dying day.

But Granny taught me something
About the way to be.
My pattern needs wrecking.
My face must be seen.

So, I've put away the mask.
No more costumes for me.
Wearing my truth ,
Shall set me free.

***

The night before the memorial service, Nadia went into Dad's room to speak to him. He had been understandably quiet and morose since his mother had passed but hadn't expressed it yet. He had busied himself with tidying up the house, informing relatives and taking care of Sabina's last rites, obviously trying to distract himself from the throbbing.

"Dad?" Nadia said, knocking on the door. "Can I come in?"

"Sure Nadia."

"Hi. How're you doing?" Nadia enquired, as she slowly entered the room. Dad was on the bed, surrounded by paper-work. Dying isn't easy business! There are a million forms to fill, insurance to claim and documents to get in order.

"I'm doing okay," he said with a sigh. "How are you doing?"

"I miss Granny. But I will be okay in time," Nadia said honestly.

"How is Rudy?"

"Oh, he is okay. Thanks!" Dad said, looking down at the papers in his hand once again.

"How come he isn't here with you?" Nadia asked, cutting to the chase. She was going to be direct from now on, like she had promised herself, even with tough conversations!

Akbar looked up, and with a wary look said, "It wouldn't be appropriate. People would ask questions."

"Not really! He is just a friend, you can say."

And then she quickly added, "Although, Dad, I do want to tell you that it would be right to tell Mom. She deserves to know. It helped me a lot, when you told me. I think it will help her too."

After a few seconds of silence, Akbar replied, "I've thought about it, Nadia. Honestly, I have. But… I'm too… ashamed. How can I tell her? She was my wife."

"I know what you mean but…you may feel better after you tell her. And I think she would take it well. I know it's a very hard thing to do, but please think about it?"

"Okay I will…but…I don't think I will change my mind Nadia," he replied frankly.

"Okay. Well don't worry. I won't tell her. It's your choice," Nadia said reassuringly, before continuing, "But Dad... I know Rudy is dying to be with you right now. Nobody will know or care. Why not let him come to Mumbai?"

"He has been saying the same thing. Nobody will even notice him at the memorial service, he says. But you know how nosey people here are."

"Yes, they are nosey, but why would they suspect anything? He is your friend, at your mother's funeral. It's not scandal material." She said the last line as a joke to lighten the mood, and it worked.

"Hmmm maybe you're right. I will have other friends there too. And Rudy will feel good to be here."

And so, the decision was made. Rudy was delighted and immediately flew to Mumbai in time for the memorial service.

I had a difficult conversation... VICTORY!

The helper and G high-fived. They knew the next lesson would require her newly-learned honesty, more than ever.

CHAPTER 22

TO BE OR...?

The morning of the memorial service, the doorbell rang at around 9 a.m. Nadia didn't pay attention to it; Aisha would open the door, she knew. Nadia was sitting in bed, sipping her morning chai while scrolling through her phone. She had tried to Facetime with Arjun that morning and last night, but hadn't gotten through to him.

Why is his phone switched off? Even my texts aren't going through.

They had never not spoken for twenty four hours, since they started talking over three months ago now.

Very odd. Maybe his phone stopped working or something...

Nadia remembered that she could call up Arjun's sister, Anya, who lived in Mumbai, to make sure he was okay.

As she picked up her phone to call Anya, there was a knock on her room door.

"Yaa..." Nadia said loudly, looking down at her phone. "Come in."

"Dee"

She recognised his voice immediately, instantly looking up.

And there he was. Their fourth encounter! Although this one, Arjun had planned.

He stood in her bedroom doorway in a white shirt and dark blue trousers, duffle bag slung across his shoulder and dimples galore. Aisha, the cook, stood behind him, having let him into the house and led him to Nadia's bedroom. On seeing Nadia's reaction to him, Aisha sensed their need for privacy, and quietly walked away.

"ARJUN!" Nadia yelled, jumping out of bed. She ran to him as he dropped his bag to the floor and hugged her. They had been waiting for this connection for a loooonng time. The dragons in her tummy had moved, they resided in her heart now, bungee jumping through her cardiovascular system to show her how much Arjun, his presence and this hug, meant to her. As if she didn't already know.

He smelled of sandal wood and musk somehow, and felt like a warm beach day. After about ten seconds of engrossed hugging, she finally had to look at him. Nadia broke the hug and stood back, still holding his hands.

"Thank you for coming!" Nadia gushed, still unable to fully comprehend that he was here, in the flesh.

"I had to see you. I had to be with you today. How are you doing?" Arjun asked, cupping her face in his hands now.

"I'm doing okay actually," she replied, sincerely, but barely able to get the words out because she was overwhelmed by his gesture- He had flown 22 hours to be with her at her grandmother's funeral.

He's a keeper all right! He came all the way for me...

"It feels surreal to see you..." Arjun said finally, reading Nadia's mind. They were just smiling and staring at each other, while holding hands now.

"Come here, I want another hug," he said, pulling her close. This time he kissed the top of her head as he held her tightly.

"Good thing I just showered," Nadia joked, while they were hugging.

Then Nadia took him by the hand and said, "Come, let me introduce you to my father."

She led Arjun to the living room where Akbar was sitting, going over his speech for the day's service. Akbar looked up and with surprise in his eyes, stood up.

"Dad, this is Arjun. From New York," Nadia said. She wasn't sure whether she should call Arjun her boyfriend or not. They hadn't established that. They hadn't even kissed yet. But he definitely was her 'someone very important'.

Dad understood though and extended his hand, "Nice to finally meet you Arjun. I was going to ask Nadia to introduce us over facetime one day, but this is much better."

"Yes it's good to meet you too," Arjun said, shaking Akbar's hand, "And I'm sorry for your loss."

"Oh thank you, Arjun. So, what brings you to town?"

"I wanted to pay my respects today. And of course to meet Nadia. But I'm only in town for five days. Didn't get more leave from work."

"Oh that's a very short trip. But it's nice of you to come. Do attend the memorial service today. I'm just headed to the airport to pick up my friend and then I'll go over there to complete some last minute preparations," Akbar said, now looking over at Nadia.

"Yes definitely. I will be there."

"Dad, you carry on. I'll see you there by three. Say hi to Rudy from me," Nadia replied, knowing her father had a lot to do that day.

"Okay, bye kids. I'll get ready and leave in ten minutes," Akbar said as he walked into his bedroom to change into white attire for the memorial service.

Nadia turned to Arjun and asked, "We still have a couple of hours till we have to head to the service. What do you want to do?"

"How about some breakfast and then you take me to your favourite spot in the city."

"Hmmm. Sounds perfect! Follow me…" and he followed Nadia into the kitchen.

They began to make fried eggs together, while Arjun told her about the guy sitting next to him on the flight who kept farting. Then Nadia read out her speech for the service to him and they ate the eggs and toast together on the dining table, laughing and holding hands, content, as if they had done this a hundred times before.

Content, except for one thing – "It sucks that you are only here for five days though!"

To which Arjun immediately replied, "Come back with me..." It almost sounded like a plea.

"I can't..." Nadia replied slowly reaching out for his hand, "I must finish my book. I've put it on pause all of last month."

"I know. But can't you finish it from there? We haven't dated while in the same city and..." Arjun broke off mid-sentence. The ending was implied – he wanted them to be together; in the same city. She knew he was right. But...

Nadia averted her eyes a little and replied, "Maybe after the book is done, I'll come for a holiday and spend some time with you. But honestly, the more I think of it, I don't see myself moving back to New York for good."

Arjun's face fell. Even as she said it, Nadia realised what it meant.

She hadn't fully realised it till just then...but she was now convinced that her life lay in Mumbai. She didn't want to leave her home. But she also hoped that her life lay with Arjun. How those two aspects could reconcile, she hadn't considered yet.

"Dee... I... I didn't know you felt that way," Arjun replied slowly pulling away his hand.

"I want to be with you. In the same city. Preferably, in the same house even," he went on frankly, looking her dead in the eyes.

"I want that too, baby. But give me some time to figure this out. Let's talk about this some more in a day or two?" she said, pulling her chair closer to his now.

And then she touched his face and said, "You make me very happy, Arjun. We can figure this out."

Which softened him and he replied, "Okay. Let's talk again in a day or two." His smile was back, though it was a little smaller now. He couldn't help but feel worried. This was not what he had expected. He had taken it for granted that after three, or four months tops, Nadia would return to NYC and they could be together, for real. She always spoke of her love for New York City. And he knew she cared for him; he felt their connection.

So what was going on? Where was this curve-ball suddenly coming from?

"Shall we go for a walk?" Nadia asked, breaking into his worried thoughts.

"Sure..." Arjun replied, standing up, his brow still a little creased with worry.

On that warm March morning, Nadia took Arjun to her favourite spot in Mumbai- Nariman Point; the southern-most tip of Marine Drive. This oceanfront drive has been informally dubbed The Queen's Necklace, for the way it lights up at night, glittering and managing to gloss over all the turmoil of the day. At night, Mumbai becomes the Queen, which she far from resembles in the harsh light of day. Though, this is precisely what most Mumbaikars love about their city- her ability to be light and dark, filthy and pure, queen and rag-picker, all at once.

The strong ocean breeze abated the morning heat a little and they walked for about 15 minutes until they reached the furthest end of the promenade. Beyond Nariman Point lay the bay, shimmering in the sunlight as the ripples on the water, shimmy-shimmied.

"This is my favourite spot," Nadia announced, when they reached the lonely tip. It would get packed with people by evening. But at 11 am on a Monday morning, it was empty, save the two of them and its native crows. Nadia and Arjun stood at the end of the promenade, surveying the view. They could see the Cuffe Parade fishing village in the distance, the peak of Afghan Church's turret jutting out from the canopy of shorter buildings around it, and the vast, calm ocean. Rising and falling, moving in and out, as it always has and always will.

"This kind of reminds me of East End Park," he said, their earlier disagreement forgotten now. "Except no cherry blossoms."

"Heyyy… We have wild almond trees though. See…" Nadia replied pointing to the row of short, leafy trees lining Marine Drive.

"That's true…" He smiled and before she knew what he was doing, he pulled her close and looked deep into her eyes.

She shut up, instantly mesmerised by the look they were sharing. And then she leaned in, as his lips met hers.

In that moment, the traffic noise, the waves, the crows ka-kawing…all of it was shut out. Even her heart slowed down, as if to stretch the minutes on longer. All her other senses went numb, while they honed in on her lips meeting his. That was all that mattered in that moment. They were in a bubble all of their own. The glorious bubble of their first kiss.

The first kiss broke, after what seemed like too short a time…so Nadia took matters into her own hands, despite her fluttering heart.

"One more…" she said, drawing him even closer this time, as they kissed again. Because one is just not enough when you have waited this long!

Finally, when they came up for air, for you can't genuinely survive on just sunshine and kisses, they both smiled, as Nadia let out a small giggle and in a soft voice said, "Yay."

"That's what she said..." Arjun joked, taking the phrase a little too literally.

"Ohh young love!" The helper sighed.

"You mean old love," G reminded him, not that he needed to. They were both familiar with Arjun and Nadia's soul connection of many, many lifetimes.

***

The last day of Arjun's Mumbai trip came before either of them could say "I wish it wasn't the last day." Arjun had attended Sabina's memorial service and watched Nadia give her speech in honour of her granny's zero f*cks given attitude. He had met her mom, dad & Rudy and she had met his sister Anya.

They had loved and chatted and cuddled and kissed incessantly for four days straight, and now on day five, with six hours to go before Arjun had to be at the airport, it was time for THE TALK. Arjun was flying back to NYC and he wanted to know when Nadia would move there and be with him. So while they lay in bed together in his hotel room that afternoon, in the after-glow moments, Arjun couldn't take it anymore and he broached the subject.

Turning to her mid cuddle, Arjun blurted out, "Dee... I want this forever. Please move back to New York. You said it yourself, we are meant to be together."

"I know, baby. I want to be with you too."

"So then move back… you can write from there. We can be together and begin our life…"

Sitting up slowly now, Nadia hesitated, then began, "Arjun, I don't know how to properly say this or explain why… but I… I don't want to move back. My family is here, this is my home, eventually I want to raise children here… not in New York, as much as I love it."

"I get that…I really do but…and I know we have only been together for four months now but… this is it for me. I want to be with you. Don't you?"

He was looking intently into Nadia's eyes now as if willing her to agree. To be with him forever. Nadia knew this to be true – He was it. But she didn't want to move… she had 'found herself' in Mumbai. And she wanted to continue living there. How could she take the risk of leaving, for good?

"I do. I really, really do. But you are asking me to move away from my home. And I don't want to, baby. How about you consider moving here?" she said clasping his fingers in hers now. "Your sister is here, you will easily get a great job here too. Your parents are close by and I know how much you miss them…and…" But he cut her off, pulling away.

"Nadia that's not fair. I have a job there and a career I've worked hard to create. I can't just give it all up and move to Mumbai right now. I won't earn half as much here, as I do in New York and you know that. Plus this isn't *my* home. You lived in New York for years, but I've never lived in Mumbai. Maybe one day we can....but for now I have to be in New York."

"But isn't it also unfair to ask me to move?" Nadia asked, getting angry now, "I know that your salary will take a hit in Mumbai. That's true...but...I want my future to be in Mumbai. I also want it to be with you. I felt like I ran away earlier and avoided my home for so long...I don't want to do that anymore, Arjun."

"I don't know what to say," Arjun replied, shocked, "I didn't know you felt like this. Sounds like you have already made up your mind. When were you going to tell me this? Or did you expect that I would just pick up and move to Mumbai, no questions asked...?" he questioned, angry, at this unexpected turn of events.

Nadia flinched. It was true. She had thought that. Bad as it sounded said out loud, she had assumed that Arjun would move to Mumbai to be with her, because he felt right and Mumbai felt right. But she hadn't considered that Mumbai may not feel right to Arjun. She hadn't considered that he could feel so vastly different from her on such an important topic. They had been on the same page about almost everything so far.

But how could she admit that to Arjun. It sounded too selfish, she realised.

"I am telling you now."

"But I asked you so many times… and you never once said you *never* wanted to move back to New York… I always thought you wanted to finish your book… or bond with your family…" Arjun yelled. He looked wounded, frustrated… like Nadia had betrayed him.

"I thought that too… but slowly I realised that I didn't want to leave. It crept up on me too Arjun… I didn't mean to hide it from you or something."

"I really don't understand this, Nadia. I love you. I know you love me. Let's just be together. It's very simple. And I promise we can consider Mumbai again at a later date," Arjun said, trying to negotiate with the woman he loved, who seemed to be slipping away.

"So what are you trying to say? That I'm purposely making it difficult?" her voice sharp now.

"I don't know. I don't know why you suddenly love Mumbai so much. It's not that great by the way. What long term future do we have here…? Look at the roads, the pollution, the crime, lack of women's rights…" Arjun had never spoken to Nadia like this before. They had never fought before, let alone like this.

"You sound like such a spoilt NRI. Every place has problems! Every city has issues, New York too. But here we have people who love us. I belong here. I never felt as at home in Boston or New York," Nadia yelled back, standing up now.

"How can you say that? You have so many friends in New York. And I'm there."

"What do you mean 'I'm there'…That's not enough. My whole life doesn't revolve around YOU!"

"I'm not saying it should, baby… but… but what about us then?" He asked, going quiet. He had stood up too but the anger had left his voice. He sounded scared now; Like he knew what was happening, but couldn't believe it.

"What about us?" Nadia replied in a biting tone that left Arjun stunned.

"So you want to live here, forever?" Arjun restated, as if hoping she would suddenly yell 'Gotcha' and reveal this was all a joke.

"Yes…" Nadia said, as a tear rolled down her cheek as she crossed her arms across her chest. As soon as she said it, she knew what that one innocuous word implied. It implied, we are over.

All of a sudden, Arjun looked like all the wind had been sucked out of him. Then, as the panic truly set in, he allowed himself to grovel, like only someone who was losing the love of their life, could do.

"Dee don't do this. Please, baby…I love you. We have to be together. There isn't another way for now Dee. Please. I promise we can return to Mumbai after a few years, but just for now…" But Nadia didn't reply. She just looked down, with no words left to give.

And Arjun looked small. Diminished. Beaten. He had seen a future with Nadia. He had hoped and loved and planned for a future, and all of a sudden, it was gone. Poof!

"How could this be happening?" he thought.

How could this be happening? she thought.

They both sat down on opposite sides of the bed, with their tears and confusion and building anger.

After twenty minutes of willing himself to get up, he finally did. Arjun put on his clothes, and packed his bag, wordlessly. He had a flight to catch.

Nadia got up too. She dressed, called her Über and pottered around the room like a robot, trying her best not to make eye contact with Arjun. Every time he looked at her, she avoided his gaze, not knowing what to say or how to make the moment any less excruciating. The reality of what had just happened, was now catching up with her and it brought with it a striking pain in her throat and a feeling of dread.

Just as Nadia turned towards Arjun & opened her mouth to speak…Arjun had already picked up his bag, and was walking out the door, without a goodbye or another look.

The door slammed shut and the words stopped short in her throat. She stood there, frozen.

She wanted to run and catch him in the hallway, kiss him, hold him tight, sob into his shirt and never let go. But she didn't. She stood there, and then when her Über arrived, Nadia went home.

And Arjun flew back to New York, speechless, tired and shattered. Had it all just been a dream?

Maybe it just wasn't meant to be.

"I guess Nadia has made her choice," G said in a quiet voice, shell shocked.

The helper didn't respond. There were no words left to say. They had done all they could and yet...

Scorched Earth
By Nadia

Why this restlessness?
Where did my inner peace go?
Did you take it with you?
I guess you reap just what you sow.

Why can't I sleep?
Even though my mind is blank.
Numb, but not asleep.
I knew the poison, yet I drank.

Why can't we be like birds?
Who migrate back and forth.
Yours and mine, could have been ours.
But the grass has burnt, the earth is scorched.

> *I keep searching for manure,*
> *To help the turf unfold.*
> *But the grass sprouts too weak to rise.*
> *I reap the disappointment I sowed.*

> *It is known! The grass is greener, when you*
> *allow it to grow.*

***

One month later, Nadia met her mother for lunch, grudgingly, for she didn't have the mental band-width to endure a probing session of "So how did you f**k up this time?" or at least that's what she thought she was getting into. But for once, she was utterly, and gloriously wrong. Roxanne had another agenda this time.

"Hi, mom… how are you?" Nadia asked with a forced smile, when Roxanne answered the door. She hadn't smiled a genuine smile in a month.

"I'm good, darling. How are you doing?" Roxanne asked immediately, as she opened the door that Sunday afternoon to let her daughter in. The house smelled of sautéing spices. Roxanne was cooking!

"I'm… Mom are you cooking?" she asked, unable to even answer her mother's question with the aroma of home cooking wafting up to her nose. Roxanne was an excellent cook but hated the heat which kitchens invariably produce. So, she seldom entered one. That Sunday afternoon, obviously, being the exception.

"Yesss," She replied with obvious pride. "I decided to make tomato par eedu for you."

"That is so sweet. Thank you, mom! I love anything par eedu. Yay."

Despite the drool-worthy aroma swirling through her brain, Nadia couldn't help but notice that many little things were different that day. Her mother hadn't immediately taken over the conversation about how bad or busy her week had been. She had actually turned the question around and asked Nadia how 'she' was doing. AND most importantly, she was cooking.

Possible reasons for this serious one eighty degree turn ran through Nadia's suspicious mind. But the most plausible seemed to be the old faithful of many, many Indian parents- She had found a boy she wanted Nadia to marry. And Nadia's break up with Arjun was the perfect opportunity to strike. Nadia decided to be on full-guard for this uncomfortable possibility.

As soon as they sat down at the dining table to eat lunch, Roxanne turned to Nadia and asked, "So how are you doing after the breakup? *Really*.....""

"Umm… it's hard but I'll be okay," Nadia replied, and then swiftly tried to change the conversation – "Oh, but I forgot to tell you. I met with my publisher yesterday and…"

But before she could say another word, Roxanne interrupted her.

"You know, I really like Arjun. I think he is a good boy."

Soooo weird! Why is mom so intent on talking about Arjun suddenly?

She didn't know how to respond, so she didn't say anything. Besides, even hearing his name hurt. After a couple of seconds of silence, Roxanne jumped right in with the million dollar question, "Why don't you want to move back to New York, Nadia?"

Clearly Roxanne was employing Nadia-esque bluntness that day!

"For Arjun? He isn't the guy I thought he was Ma," Nadia said, after being caught thoroughly off guard by this line of questioning.

"What do you mean?"

"He isn't *all* that nice…"

Nadia went on, "I guess it just took me time to see. But he showed me his true colours after all. After we had that fight and essentially broke up, he just went back to New York. And then he wrote me this long and ridiculously mean email. Who does that? It's like he just wanted to hurt me."

"What does it say?" Roxanne asked, seeming pained by this news.

By now, Nadia couldn't hold the grief in any longer, and she began to weep. The anguish just flowed out.

"I couldn't believe what I was reading, mom. He calls me selfish and says I lied to him and led him on. He says that I played mind games with him and that he wishes he had never met me. I couldn't believe that the man I loved for so many months, could say these things to me. It's like the love switch just turned off in his heart. It was so…venomous."

Roxanne looked genuinely sad hearing all of this. She took a second and then leaned in and held Nadia's hand while she wept, the food in their plates, completely forgotten.

"Baby, why do you think he sent you that email?"

After some thought, and through the tears Nadia responded honestly, "To punish me. To hurt me like I hurt him."

"I think you are right. We all do horrible things when we are hurt," Roxanne said, with a hint of regret in her voice.

"And the worst part is… I still miss him. Even after reading his…" Nadia just trailed off. She wished she could just feel okay. But after losing granny, and now Arjun, Nadia felt lost. Lost in the hurricane of her mind which swirled and twirled around violently all day. She felt like she was wandering, and there weren't any mile markers or North stars to guide her, and no hope of feeling un-lost.

"You miss him because you love him." For once, Roxanne was spot on.

"I do."

"Then why didn't you want to move to New York, jaan?" Roxanne asked gently for a second time. Her voice was soft and yet determined. She wanted an answer.

"I… I kind of knew something like this would happen, to be honest. And then what would I do? I'd be in New York, for a guy. What would that say about me? How un-feminist!"

"So you didn't go there because you knew you two would break up?"

"In a way… I mean, problems eventually come up right? And I didn't want to put my life on hold and then be left with nothing, when shit hits the fan."

"But why are you certain you would eventually break up? You love him right ? And I think he loves you."

Roxanne couldn't understand this doom and gloom logic, Nadia was, all of a sudden, employing.

"Because life is uncertain, mom. Shit happens all the time. That's just how it is! Look at you and dad. Anything can happen to a relationship… to a person. Love isn't enough. And I didn't want to be foolish and risk everything and regret it years later."

She stopped and neither of them said anything.

Roxanne hadn't known Nadia felt that way. Nadia hadn't fully known that Nadia felt that way! That she felt this hopeless about life and love. She always portrayed the exact opposite.

"Now her truth is out, so she can unpack it," The helper said, relieved that the curtain of ignorance had been lifted by Nadia' s words.

Roxanne continued to look flabbergasted while Nadia's words sank into her brain.

Finally, seeing her mother quiet for so long, Nadia tried to end the conversation by saying, "And look, I was right. He has been so cruel to me these last few weeks. I'm just going to put this behind me, mom. Don't worry."

Slowly, Roxanne decided to say something. She couldn't let her daughter lose the most important thing she had ever had – hope.

She carefully formed her reply and began, "Nadia, I don't know too much about your relationship, and maybe you are right and he isn't the one for you. But… can I tell you something I've learned over the years?"

"What?" Nadia asked tentatively.

"Everyone hurts the people they love."

Nadia blinked. The words penetrated.

Then Roxanne went on, "But that doesn't mean you can just stop loving them. Yes, Arjun has hurt you, and you hurt him too. But being with someone takes sacrifice, and leaps of faith sometimes. And you know what? You are so, so strong. If anyone can take this leap of faith, it's you. If anyone can choose to love, despite fear and hurt, it's you. If anyone can work at building a life with someone, it's you."

She paused, but then spoke on, "Don't make the mistakes I did, Nadia. Don't let fear control you."

"But Mom…"

"Just think about what I've said okay?"

Stunned, Nadia just muttered an 'Okay'. Her mother had never been this vulnerable with her before. She couldn't deny the power of Roxanne's words, for they had calmed the mental hurricane in her. Her thoughts weren't circling and colliding in her brain anymore. Now, she was only thinking about one thing —

Am I letting fear control me? Is mom right?

For the rest of the day, Nadia thought over this one question.

And the answer ringing true in her heart, pained her. *YES.* She was afraid. She was scared of failing at life.

She was scared of ending up with the wrong person.

She was scared that even if Arjun was the right person, she would drive him away.

She was afraid of making nothing of herself.

She was petrified of getting hurt.

She knew that moving to New York would mean Arjun was it- THE ONE. She would essentially be locking it down with him and her heart pounded and her palms sweated at that prospect.

What if, like most people, I screw up too? What if it's all a huge mistake?

All these fears had led her to fight with and walk away from Arjun.

Realizing all these fears, hit Nadia like a tidal wave. She felt pummelled by all the fears that secretly lived in her and had only recently showed themselves. All this thinking eventually made her head start to ache. The headache got stronger and stronger over the next hour.

Nadia tried to distract herself by watching her favourite comic relief- Seinfeld. Usually, George Costanza's antics could distract her from absolutely anything, but on that day, the headache only worsened. Several aspirins didn't work. A cold shower didn't work. Crying for stress-relief, didn't work.

Finally, Nadia just lay down in bed and tried to focus on her breath, to take her mind off the throbbing in her temples. No thoughts. Only breath.

She breathed in and out, in and out, in and out... and slowly her thoughts drifted away from how beaten by life she felt.

Her thoughts drifted to Chris. She thought about a rainy hike up Overlook Mountain they had done, one summer Sunday in the Catskill area. It had rained all the way up, but they kept going because they knew the eventual view would be spectacular. And they had been right.

Due to the rain, there was no one else around when they reached the summit. They had spent almost an hour up there, admiring the view and the silence. What a happy memory it was! Thinking of that hike, and how they had laughed and talked and sang that day made Nadia smile. She could even almost smell the rain and the moss that coated the rocks at the top. She noticed her headache reducing and her heart rate slowing down.

Thinking of Chris, always made her grateful for having had him in her life, even though he wasn't around anymore. As she thanked God, for the umpteenth time, for blessing her with her best friend, Nadia realised something. Had she known Chris was going to die, would she have preferred to never have met him? It would have definitely saved her many years of pain and anguish.

Would I have chosen to not know Chris at all?

NEVER.

It wasn't even an option.

Chris's importance wasn't diminished by his death.

So then, how can Arjun's importance be diminished by the possibility of it not working out with him?

Nadia realised that she couldn't run scared. That would be the biggest disservice to herself! She had to play the game, to find out if she could win. She had to try. The time for baby steps, had passed.

Wow. Mom was right!

"There's a phrase I know Nadia never thought she would say," G said with glee.

260

The helper chuckled too. Planting the seed through Roxanne had been his idea.

***

At 4:06 am that night, Nadia sent an email to Arjun. She hadn't responded to his earlier angry email, but now she knew what she wanted to say and most importantly, she had worked up the courage to say it.

Dear Arjun,

I'm writing to tell you that I was wrong. I pushed you away and I wish I hadn't, but I can't go back and change it. You probably hate me now and don't want to be with me but I have to tell you the truth.

The truth is – I love you.

The other truth is – I'm scared.

I love you because you are kind, caring, funny, thoughtful and you never once (unlike me) doubted that we are meant to be together. I love you because of your faith in me and in us.

I am scared because I can't seem to fully let go of the hurt of the years, and I've almost come to expect it. Since I expect hurt, I have to guard myself against it and that is why I pushed you away. I didn't agree to move to New York, not because I don't love you enough, but because (in my own misguided way) I was trying to protect myself.

I'm truly sorry for having caused you this pain and if it's any consolation, I feel it too, along with guilt and fear.

But I also feel hope, and love, and it is starting to overshadow the fear. Day by day, the love and hope in me grow, and they are eclipsing the fear. I'm certain that soon I'll be able to jump into life, without the safety net of self-sabotage, because I will have that much love for myself, and hope for my life. The fear may not completely go away, but it's power over me, already is.

That wouldn't have happened if not for you. In fact, I didn't even realise I was so afraid, until you came along. So thank you for showing me a part of myself that was hiding deep inside, and for giving me so much love, comfort, joy and happiness over these six months.

Arjun, I love you immensely and I want to be with you, in New York, or wherever else you want. I am ready to build a life with you. I'm ready to jump. I know that life will continue to challenge us and there will be many, many difficult times we will have to face. For this reason, I promise you that I will never again respond to you out of fear. I will never again let my fear win over my love.

I know that maybe you have moved on and don't want 'us' anymore, but a girl can hope...

With all my love,

Nadia

***

Love is...

By Nadia

We war for the ones we Love,
Clawing at their walls till our fingernails
break.
Through wounds and gashes,
Betrayals and disappointments,
We never give up.
For to Love, is to breach.

We wipe the slate clean
For the ones we love.
We crack open for them,
And let our hearts hope
Once again. Just once more.
For to love, is to forget.

All is forgotten, for Love.
All is forgiven, for Love.
All is forsaken, for Love.

Our depths were created for Love.
It pulls us in, as we push it out.
Love has entwined us, and now we can't get
un-tangled.
In misguided times we sometimes try and
comb away the knot,
But thankfully, it doesn't budge. It cannot.
For to Love, is a must.

CHAPTER 23

THE END

Nadia looked into the mirror and saw the contentment of the years in her eyes.

She didn't even notice the wrinkles around her eyes, the sagging skin of her neck, the scanty white hair on her head and how her nose, once proud and long, now drooped, low with age.

For years, she would look into this mirror to observe and marvel at how the ageing process was steadily changing her exterior. She had to keep re-acquainting herself with the Nadia in the mirror.

Is there anything I would have done differently? she thought that day. The answer was a resounding no, which filled her with gratitude while she sat in their faded-ivory coloured bedroom.

The décor was sparse and uncluttered. There was a full length mirror on the wall, a chair in front of it, and a bookshelf on the wall behind her. On the far right, by the windows, was their large bed. The wardrobes were to her left, by the door of the bedroom. The bookshelf was filled with books, little knick-knacks from their travels over the years, and family photos.

One of the photos was of the two of them on their wedding day, youthful and all smiles. Arjun was sweating like a man who had just run a marathon, while Nadia looked up at his face. Their daughter loved this picture because it looked funny, as if Nadia was just a little grossed out by, but mostly bonkers in love with her new husband.

There was a picture of the first ocean clean-up drive Nadia had spearheaded. Since then, she had assembled groups all of over Mumbai, almost every Saturday to clean the crowded beaches of the city they called home.

There was a picture of their daughter, Sara, beaming on her graduation day in her cap and gown. And then there was a picture of the three of them that they had taken, just last year, on their visit to NYC, sitting under the cherry blossoms at East End Park. Sara had insisted on it because she had heard the story of her parents first meeting many, many times and had wanted to revisit the spot and document it.

Behind the curios and photo-frames, stood some of their favourite books and of course, the books Nadia had authored over the years. There was her first one Food for Thought, that chronicled her best and worst memories and the recipes of the food associated with them. Then, stood her next book Food for Two, a guide to quick and easy recipes for couples on the go, with a passion for eating, but not too much time to spend on complex culinary pursuits.

Her third book was the one she had written after they had moved back to Mumbai from NYC. She had decided to learn tarot from Susan and this book was a beginner's guide to the symbolism behind the tarot cards. Then, there were two poetry books Nadia had ultimately published after working up the courage to share her inner world with others. Nadia's sixth and final book was her favourite so far – Baking with my Baby. It contained recipes of baked goods that were meant to be made together by parent and child. Nadia and Sara had spent many Sunday hours baking, eating and experimenting with cupcakes, brownies, madeleines, pies and all things sweet. That was how Arjun had developed the slight paunch he now had.

The poetry, cookbooks, beach clean-up drives and the tarot she had practiced, represented much more than just professions for Nadia. They represented the journey of her life, her contribution.

"Thank you for your never ending help G," Nadia said, feeling full of love.

"I'm always with you," G replied, though she still couldn't hear him.

The Reset had been worth it!

God turned to The helper, "Our work here seems to be done."

"Okay! Next birth time?" The helper asked matter-of-factly for they were well aware of the order of life — a constant cycling and recycling of memory and matter.

"Let's bring her home," G decided.

The helper obliged.

With the blink of an eye, the aroma of roses filled the air and Nadia left her body... in the next instant, the three long lost friends were together again, and began to plan and plot her next journey on the spiralling cosmic highway.

THE END (Not really)

SIDE NOTE

Hi earth folk,

This is The helper here. I thought I would clue you in to Nadia's old story – the pre-Reset one – so you know why we gave her a second chance.

You see, her soul had chosen to learn a couple of lessons as 'Nadia'. But as happens many a time, after being born, everyday life and all its distractions, took over. She lost her way and strayed further and further away from her learnings.

Nadia ignored her instincts, and us, and chose to stay on in a career she had never liked. She never wrote the books she could have, never explored tarot and never built up enough gusto to organize the beach clean-ups.

She also chose to marry Zaal. Zaal chose to continue to be the person he was and their marriage was unhappy and contentious, and eventually ended. Nadia didn't move forward after this, choosing to move further away from love and compassion. She became a recluse.

She never got to the point of trying to mend with her parents and their relationship remained distant and closed off till they both passed away, leaving Nadia with weighty regret and bitterness. The bitterness build up made Nadia lose her love for life which life didn't like, and threw more sorrow Nadia's way. Eventually at seventy six, she reached rock bottom, her own personal hell.

That day, when she looked into the mirror, she spoke to us after almost twenty years! Her agony pushed our hand.

Also, in that moment Nadia suddenly realised one crucial thing- she hadn't used her courage. Realising that, helped her. It let us give her a second chance.

That's why G did what he usually never does. G let her reset and work on the same life, once again. And we are so kicked she was successful the second time round. Phew! Mission accomplished.

GLOSSARY OF TERMS

1. Parsi – Refers to the Persian community of Zoroastrians who now live in India. Between the 8th and 10th century CE, to avoid persecution following the Arab conquest of Persia, Zoroastrians (followers of the Zoroastrian Faith) fled from Iran to India. There are around 60,000 Parsis in Mumbai.

2. Dhaping – fibbing in Hindi

3. ICSE and ISC- A very important 10th grade exam that is conducted all over India. ICSE stands for 'Indian Certificate of Secondary Education'

4. Chai – Tea

5. Desi – An Indian or anyone from the Indian subcontinent.

6. Goa – Goa is a tiny state on the west coast of India known for tourism and an influx of foreigners who flock to it for its beaches, warm weather and laid-back lifestyle.

7. Biryani – It is a South Asian mixed rice dish with Muslim origins. It is famous all of over India.

8. Gulab – Rose. Gulabo is an Indian version of the name Rosie.

9. Ice-gola – Ice popsicles.

10. Khali-khali – Hindi word for Empty.

11. Bai – Female house-help.

12. Chor-police – This is the Indian version of the game cops and robbers. It is commonly played all over India as a variant of hide and go seek

13. Farchas – deep fried chunks of any meat; A typically Parsi dish.

14. NRI – Acronym for 'Non-Resident Indian'

15. Eedu – Eggs

16. Par eedu – Any food item prepared 'with eggs' (refers to commonly prepared Parsi dishes made from eggs and almost anything else e.g. tomatoes, potatoes, okra etc. etc.)

17. Mumbaikars – Residents of Mumbai

18. Jaan – 'my love' in Urdu

THE CHARACTERS IN NADIA'S LIFE

Roxanne – Mother

Akbar – Father

Sabina – Paternal Grandmother

Payal – Childhood friend

Jay – High School boyfriend

Siya – Girl from the 'cool gang' in High School

Tara – Roommate in college

Isla – Roommate in college

Zack – Date in college

Chris – Best Friend

Gabby – Chris's girlfriend

Connie – Work-wife at eWay

Zaal – Boyfriend

Riya – Zaal's ex-fiancé

Gulabo – Childhood Nanny

Susan – Tarot Card Reader

Rudy – Father's Partner

Arjun – The One

Aisha – Sabina's cook

Anya – Arjun's sister

Sara – Nadia and Arjun's daughter